TOUCHE

ASYLUM

JESSICA LYNCH

FOREWORD

Asylum is the first of three books that will tell the story of a young woman named Riley Thorne. While it is a supernatural series, full of magic, mayhem, adventure, prophecies, and romance, it also features some real world issues, too.

Because of the way the Black Pine facility is designed—it's a home for "wayward juveniles"—nearly every in-patient grapples with their own issues. So, please, consider this a content warning for mental health, doctors, eating disorders, and more. Riley's official diagnosis is schizotypal personality disorder because of her insistence that fae are real—and they're after her. That colors this whole first book.

Of course, as you read the series, you learn that that is true. The fae *are* after her, but that doesn't diminish her last six years of recovery inside of the asylum. Or the phobias she developed along the way.

I wanted to give readers the opportunity to make an

informed decision about whether or not this is the type of book for them. If you choose to continue, I hope you enjoy the first part of Riley's journey!

And, as a reminder, the prequel to *Asylum*, *Favor*, is currently out now if you would like to read about just why the fae are after Riley in the first place.

xoxo,
Jessica

SHE'S DESTINED TO STAY
MORE THAN A LOVER,
    A CONSORT, A FRIEND
WHEN DARK MATTS SHADOW
THE REIGN OF THE DAMNED
    SHALL COME TO AN END

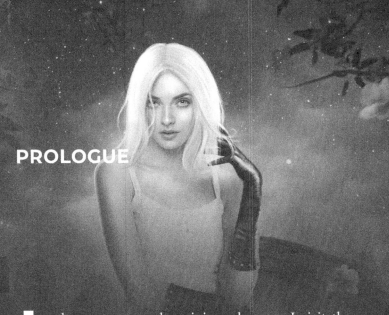

PROLOGUE

I t always seems to be raining whenever I visit the cemetery.

Just my luck. Within minutes, I'm already soaked. I wish my shirt had a hood, something, anything to cover my head. No dice. Despite the year-round air conditioning in my room, I always sleep in a basic tee; it's the only time I can let the bare skin of my arms go uncovered. My favorite hoodie is probably right where I left it: tossed on top of my dresser. If it wasn't for the chilly rain, I wouldn't need it.

I know every inch of this place. I mean, I've spent more than enough time here. I head toward the closest mausoleum. The name on the outside says Richardson, and it's got the widest overhang on this side of the cemetery. I duck beneath it, shrinking against the marble in a fruitless attempt to avoid the raindrops. They're falling hard and fast, plopping against the flattened grass, spraying dots of mud against the hem of my pajama pants.

A light bobs in the distance. Up. Down. Up. Down. I follow the white splotch as it moves further out. It's the caretaker, making his last rounds of the night. The glowing blob of light? His lantern going on the journey with him.

I know the old guy's routine almost as well as he does. First, he'll check to make sure no one is stupid enough to be caught on the grounds this late at night— especially during another summer storm—then he'll head back inside, lock up his office, close the gates, and go home.

My eyes trained on the moving light, I keep to the shadows where I know he won't find me. The shadows have always protected me. I'm safe here.

Not that I can explain *how* I got here. Hell, I don't even know how I'm going to make my way back. Acorn Falls is about a half an hour away from Black Pine by car—and I never learned to drive. On foot? Hours, easy.

That's okay. The cemetery tonight? This is where I'm supposed to be. It's where I belong.

Closing my eyes, I listen to the pitter-patter of the raindrops hitting the graves around me. The wind screams and howls and I stay tensed, waiting for the clap of thunder or the crash of lightning. A storm's brewing all right. When I open my eyes again, there's hardly any difference. It's too dark to make out anything now that the lantern is so far away.

It's only growing colder out, too. I hug myself,

pulling my thin t-shirt close, shivering when the clammy tips of my leather gloves cut right through the soaked material. The rain has washed the rest of the day's warmth right away. A few strokes shy of midnight, I'm almost freezing. It doesn't help that the marble of the mausoleum leeches any body heat I've got left.

Still, I refuse to leave.

Not yet.

The storm is my friend. Eager to get out of the rain, the cemetery caretaker half-asses his job. His luck is a tiny bit better than mine and he manages to shine his light back in my direction without even meaning to before glancing away. Like every other time I've inexplicably found myself at this cemetery, he doesn't know I'm here.

Phew. I'm just glad that the mausoleum shields me while the shadows hide me. It was a close call. When he shifts again, I let out a sigh of relief between chattering teeth.

His lantern is nothing but a pinprick in the distance as he moves further and further away. Suddenly, the light is gone.

I wait a few minutes more. My teeth won't stop chattering and I'm damn lucky that I don't slice off a piece of my tongue when it slips between my molars. Inside my gloves, I can feel my fingers becoming prunes; the water always finds a way to seep in. I find myself wishing I had a napkin or a towel. For too long I had to be careful to keep my brand new hands dry. All these years later, it's a reflex. I guess it's just too hard of a habit to break.

When I hear the roar, I think the thunder has arrived. That's before twin lights turn on and break up the gloom. Headlights. The caretaker has started his beater of a truck. I duck down, making myself even smaller as I press my back up against the mausoleum. My skin is white, my pale blonde hair a few shades lighter. Even though my t-shirt is black—my gloves, too —if he peeks this way again and I'm not hiding, no way he'll miss me.

The marble is so cold that it feels like I've been stabbed. I hiss through my teeth, but I don't move away from the wall until I see the truck lurch toward the front gate. Mud sucks at the tires. The car whines as he surges forward, stopping when he reaches the opposite side of the entrance.

The caretaker keeps his truck running while he jumps out and yanks the gate closed. He locks it, trapping me in the cemetery with my demons and my ghosts.

I let out another soft sigh of relief. To be honest, I much prefer it that way.

Madelaine's grave is located on the west end of the cemetery, not too far from the Richardsons' mausoleum. Balling my hands into fists inside the squishy gloves, I push off of the mausoleum's outer wall and step lightly onto the flooded grass. It's slick and slippery. I come close to falling a couple of times. Once, I nearly lose my slipper in a deceiving puddle. I grit my teeth and keep on going. I don't know how I got here, but I know why I've come.

It's little more than a drizzle when I find the right resting place.

The Everetts marked her grave with a giant stone angel. It's hard to miss, but I run my gloved fingers along each wing, recognizing the carved lines and the chip on the right side. Almost six years later, through the rain and sleet and the snow, and that chip is still the same size.

I hardly pay any attention to the rain, the damp ground, even the chill as I kneel in front of her grave. Moving my hand lower, I trace each letter in her name until I'm satisfied that I'm with my sister again. I turn so that I'm sitting on the marble base, resting my back against her headstone.

There are no words. I sit in silence, my head bowed into my chest.

It's only when the rain quits at last and the sky starts to lighten that I wonder if anyone from the asylum has noticed that I'm gone.

CHAPTER 1

The first thing I see when I open my eyes again is my window. Six bars stretch vertically across the lengths of the glass plane. And it hits me.

I'm not at the cemetery. I'm back at Black Pine again.

The *asylum*.

Breathing in deep, I can't get the smell of wet grave-yard soil out of my nose. My bangs are plastered down to my forehead, but it has to be sweat. I mean, there's no way that I actually could have left my room.

I haven't been on the outside in close to six years.

I shove my bangs back. They squelch against my leather gloves. I can't stop my shudder. Getting my gloves wet is even worse than when I'm forced to bare my hands in front of an audience. My stomach was already queasy from a poor night's sleep full of vivid dreams and bad memories. The damp leather gloves make it so much worse.

Might as well get up. There's no chance in hell I can even think about going back to sleep now.

That's nothing new. Not for me. I always wake up before seven. I can't remember the last time I was jerked from my sleep by the facility's wake-up calls. Not since I stopped taking my sleeping medication regularly, I bet. More often than not, I'm up and dressed before the morning tech knocks on my door and tells me it's time to get going. Most days I even have my bed made.

After all this time, I know the routine.

Amy is peppy, a real morning person. Today she chatters about her most recent attempt at potty-training her son while she checks my vitals. Blood pressure, pulse, temperature... she seamlessly goes from one test to the next, marking the results down on my chart. Once she pronounces me fit as a fiddle, she sends me off for my morning meds and my shower.

A blonde technician I don't recognize is standing in front of the chalkboard at the nursing station. She writes the morning message quickly before hurrying off, wiping the chalk dust from her hands onto her scrubs. A faint white ghost hand leaves a trail down the side of her light blue pants.

I turn to look at the board. It says the same sort of thing it usually does, for those who can't remember:

Today is Sunday. You are at Black Pine Facility for

Wayward Juveniles. This is the residential ward for the 19-21 age group. It is raining outside. All windows must remain shut.

I feel better knowing that it's raining out. That explains part of my dream, even if I still can't figure out why my hair was so damp. Leaving it at sweat, I snort at that last line.

This technician must be new to Black Pine if she thinks we can open any of the windows here. Despite its stupid name, we all know that the asylum—sorry, Facility for Wayward Juveniles—is really more of an old-fashioned, obsolete psych hospital. Come on. We're on the fifth floor. They're not going to risk us jumping. None of these windows open.

It's sad, in a way. Last night's dream makes me remember how much I miss the fresh air. If I breathe in deep, I can still smell the damp earth and the rain on the marble gravestones.

Shit.

I've got to remember not to tell any of my doctors about that. If they think my hallucinations are stretching to different senses, who knows what they'll prescribe for me next. All I *do* know is that I'm pretty sure I can't stomach any more medication.

Speaking of medication—

Three other patients are already lined up at the nursing station, waiting for their morning meds. Since Amy started at our end of the floor, it's all girls. Our crew will be the first in the showers, too. Sometimes I suspect that Amy does it on purpose, waking the girls up first so that we get that extra half an hour to use the showers before the boys do, but she's never said. Then again, I've never asked.

I learned a long time ago not to bother asking any questions. People lie. It's what they do. And, hell if I know why, but I've always been able to tell. It gets depressing after a while. I've gotten used to tuning it out, even if I can't turn it off entirely.

Carolina brings up the rear, her long dark hair a curtain as she nibbles on her thumbnail. I get in line right behind her, trying not to notice just how loosely her Black Pine tee hangs off her bony frame. She's the most recent chick to join our floor. New meat, too, not one of the kids on the fourth floor who aged out to ours. She's quiet, seems sweet, and even if she didn't open up during group therapy, I'd still have a pretty good idea why her parents tossed her inside with the rest of us.

When she senses me lingering a couple of steps behind her, she shoves her sheet of hair over her shoulder, her eyes friendly as she grins over at me. Nope. I immediately drop my gaze to the tiles. They're a pristine white speckled with grey, and though I've seen them every day for the last two years, they're suddenly the most fascinating tiles in the world.

I mean, look at that speckle over there. With the shadow and the shape, it reminds me of a dolphin. And that one—

Carolina lets out a soft sigh, then shuffles so that she's facing the front of the nurse's station again.

I want to tell her that I can't help it. That it's not just her, either.

I don't.

I can't.

Besides, if she's locked up in here with me long enough, she'll learn. Unable to form personal relationships, abandonment issues, a deep-seated fear that everyone I've ever known or loved will eventually leave me… that's why I'm at Black Pine.

Well, those are *some* of the reasons why I'm committed here.

The line moves quickly. Our morning nurses are quick and efficient. It's their job, them and the techs, to make sure that us juveniles have a strict routine and that we stick to it.

Before we're even up, the medicines have already been doled out into individual dixie cups with our names scribbled on the side in black marker. When it's my turn, I step up to the nursing station. Already looking past me to the next in line, the nurse hands me the cup that says **R. Thorne**.

I peek inside, giving the cup a shake. Four pills roll around the bottom, just like every morning. Since there's no point arguing with the nurse, I toss them back before moving aside and making room for Meg. I chase my meds with one of the apple juice cups left out on a tray. The bitter taste still lingers on my tongue.

Ugh. No matter how long I've been doing this, I've always hated this part.

Too bad there's nothing I can do about it.

In other facilities, patients are allowed to refuse their meds. Not me, and not most of us at Black Pine. It's one thing if you voluntarily stick yourself inside, but nearly everyone I've met in my six years here has been tossed in by someone else. A mother. A grandfather. Maybe an aunt, uncle, or a second cousin twice removed, I don't know. Because we come here when we're minors, it's usually the adults that make the call.

In my case, the state has control of me. It was either here or prison, and even if *I* don't think I'm crazy, I would have to be if I picked prison over the asylum. When I turn twenty-one in two weeks, I'm finally free of this place.

That means I only had to do six years. If I chose prison, the sentence for manslaughter is almost fifteen.

AFTER I SHOWER AND CHANGE INTO FRESH clothes, I head off to breakfast.

There are two tables in the dining area: one for the girls, another for the guys. I must have taken longer to wash up than usual because I'm the last chick to take her assigned seat. The guys start to trickle in about ten minutes later, filling up their table. When it seems like we're missing someone, I do a quick headcount. Twelve. Someone's not here.

It takes me a second before I realize it's Jason, a tall, light-skinned black boy who always had an optimistic outlook. He's still not here when the morning techs announce that it's time to eat. I vaguely wonder what happened to him. I'm the oldest in our ward, so close to twenty-one that I can almost taste it, so he hasn't moved on before me.

Maybe he's been released. Maybe he's in trouble and they're keeping him confined to his room. I give it another few seconds of thought, then let it slip away.

In-patients change. Techs change. Doctors change. All that matters is that I'm still here.

For two weeks, three days, and a couple of hours longer, I'm stuck inside.

I can not *wait* to get out.

At least it's Sunday. Sundays are way easier than most other days. Because it's the weekend, our schedule is a bit more lenient. Yeah, we still have to get up ass early, but we get an hour for breakfast, then another hour to just kind of unwind before sessions start.

I won't see any of my doctors today—not until Monday—but there's Lorraine, my social worker, who I see once a week because the courts say I have to, my mandatory daily check-in, plus group therapy. It's usually art on Sundays. Actually, it's art therapy most rainy days. Or whenever the facility staff runs out of ideas for us.

Whatever.

On the plus side, Sunday is pancake day. It's a treat. Something to look forward to.

Of course, not everyone is happy. In her high-pitched whine, Whitney complains that she's allergic to chocolate and all of the pancakes are contaminated. She insists that Amy throw the whole tray out, pouting when Amy whips out her clipboard with her notes on it and reminds her that Whitney's only allergens on file are cat dander and pollen. Because she's used to Whitney's complaints—she pulls this same stunt every Sunday—Amy offers Whitney a blueberry pancake instead, but Whitney scowls and jerks her plate closer to her.

Chocolate it is.

I drop two blueberry pancakes on my own plate. After I cover them in butter—no syrup for me, the pancakes are sweet enough—I start to chow down. I'm not big on interacting with the others, for obvious reasons, but I guess you could say I'm a people-watcher. As I eat, I look around the room.

Carolina has the seat across from me. She isn't eating, I notice. She just rips her pancake up into smaller pieces before pushing the pieces around her plate. If you weren't watching her, it would seem as if she'd eaten some of it. If you weren't watching, or if you didn't know any better.

I'm not the only one who sees that. Standing back, clipboard up as she keeps an eye on our breakfast table, Amy frowns. Grabbing a pen from her pocket, she makes a note on the clipboard. That sucks for Carolina.

She probably just lost another point for that and, since she's a new case, that might mean another day committed.

Poor kid.

Slap.

Everyone looks over at the boy's table, including me. Vinnie, an excitable white guy with spiky black hair, is standing up, his hand outstretched. Considering Tai is sitting across from Vinnie, syrup glistening on his cheek, half of a pancake stuck to the side of his throat, it doesn't take a super genius to figure out what happened.

That's when Whitney lets out a shrill shout.

"*Food fight!*"

It doesn't get any further than that. Amy tosses her clipboard onto the dining cart, Louis already rushing forward to settle down the guys. I roll my eyes at their antics. Once you make it to this floor, we're supposed to be adults. No one here is younger than eighteen, but I get why we're still considered *wayward juveniles*. A food fight? Seriously?

That's a waste of good pancakes.

While Amy and Louis work on separating Vinnie from a furious Tai, I peek over at Carolina. Both tables are too involved in what's going on over on the boys' side to notice the way that she's staring wistfully at the food on her plate. It's like she wants to eat, only she can't bring herself to.

I think of Amy's clipboard and the note she left on Carolina's chart. Before anyone can catch me, I reach out and snatch one of the largest chunks of pancakes from her plate. Her dark brown eyes light up in relief when she realizes what I've done—and why I've done it.

She gives me a grateful smile.

I want to smile back. I really do. She's new, but Carolina seems nice, and it's not as if I've got too many friends already that I don't have time for any more. If there's one thing I learned, though, it's that people come and people go.

I *want* to smile. I can't. I don't. Instead, I shove the whole piece of pancake in my mouth. Oops. Can't be friendly if I'm too busy chewing on a pancake. Sorry.

Once I finish that piece, I focus on my plate. The butter is a melty, delicious mess. Sure, it drips a little, leaving a shiny, oily streak on my right glove that's barely discernible among the other scratches and marks. That's what happens when you wear leather gloves around the clock. I've already stained them with everything under the sun. What's one more streak?

Today's pancakes are delicious. I put my two away before I feel a little full and decide against a third. Amy nods encouragingly as she gives me the okay to get rid of my garbage.

I've given up trying to explain that, unlike Carolina and some of the asylum's other "guests", food has never been a problem for me. My appearance, either. That surprises some of my doctors. With all of the problems they insist I have, poor body image isn't one of them. So many of the kids here hate the way they look.

Not me. I never have.

Well, except for my hands. But that makes sense to the professionals. There's a reason behind that—and it doesn't have anything to do with the things I used to see, or the voices I heard when I was a kid.

CHAPTER 2

Of us all, Dean is the grumpiest after breakfast. Definitely not a morning person. If the techs let him, he'd easily sleep until noon. Of course, the techs never let him. It would go against our routine and, oh boy, that's just not going to happen. But Louis does have to resort to threatening Dean's television privileges to get him up and ready before we eat.

Whether it's spite or his grumpy nature, Dean retaliates by taking forever to finish his meal. He's usually the last one to come slinking into the day room, the common area where we all kind of gather together when we're not in session or confined to our rooms.

Today's the same as every other day. Routine, right? By the time Dean joins us, most of the chairs are already occupied, especially the ones closest to the screen. I've staked out my perch on one of the sofas, leaning into the far side, careful to keep enough space between Kim and me so that we don't accidentally bump into each other.

The television is tuned to some kiddy channel. It always is on the weekend. It doesn't matter that most of our group grew out of Spongebob and My Little Pony years ago. This is a juvenile facility, the kids inside ranging from six to twenty-one. I'm used to it, and I barely pay attention to the laughter coming from the screen.

Now that we're enjoying our free time, I think about this morning. About the scent of graveyard soil in my nose, and the way my bangs lay plastered to my sweaty forehead.

My dreams—when I have them—are weird. That wasn't the first time I fell asleep and dreamed of returning to a place that I should be staying far away from. I wish I could blame my nighttime meds, but I know it's not them; my sleeping pills make it so that I can't dream. Still, it's super weird. I mean, who *wants* to spend their nights in an empty cemetery?

Well, except for me, I guess. When I'm sleeping, at least.

But when I'm awake?

I… I don't know what I would do.

I'm gonna find out soon, though.

Two weeks, three days, and a couple of hours until freedom. That's all I'm looking forward to. Two weeks, three days, and a couple of hours until Lorraine signs off on my file and I start the next phase of my life. I'm not sure what's next, but I know one thing: it's better than sitting around in Black Pine. Lately, I can't help but think of this place as a hellish kind of limbo. I think I've learned everything I'm going to, I haven't had an episode in years, and if I dream about leaving the asylum after hours, at least I know it's just a result of my overactive imagination.

I mean, there are *bars* on my window. How could I sneak out—or come back without anyone realizing it?

Dean shuffles into the day room, muttering to himself as he does. It never makes any sense—not to anyone but Dean, anyway—and I zone him out, too, until he plops his wide body in the gap left between me and Kim.

Suddenly, I'm paying super close attention.

It seems to happen in slow motion. The couch gives a small bounce at his weight, my body jolting just enough to shift sideways. His Black Pine t-shirt clips the side of my left hand. I sense the faint brush of fabric against the edge of my glove. My reaction is as immediate as it is over the top: my whole body stiffens for a heartbeat before I jerk and leap away, desperate to put some space between us.

One problem with that. I must have been sitting on the edge of the seat or something because, when I jump, I end up in a pile on the floor. Like, my ass slides right off before hitting the carpet with a muffled *thump*.

Pain shoots up my spine. I ignore it. All I can think about is how close Dean came to brushing his arm against mine.

Just like I'm used to the other kids' quirks, they've all

seen me at my worst. A couple of months ago, I was banned from the day room for seven straight days because I swung a remote at Jeffrey all because he thought it would be funny to stand in front of me, his hand extended, mockingly repeating, "I'm not touching you, I'm not touching you," over and over again. I missed, since I didn't want to get too close, but I lost a couple of points for that fight.

It was worth it.

Dean didn't do it on purpose. I know he didn't.

Now if only I could convince myself that.

Because they're used to me reacting like this, none of the other patients do anything to help me. It would only make things worse. The last thing I need right now? A panic attack. I don't get as many now that my meds are regulated, but when I *do* get them, they come fast and terrible.

I can already tell my heart is racing. My breath is short, my body tight. I feel like I just missed getting hit by a car.

That's what Dean's touch feels like to me. Like a car accident.

I try to take a deep breath and choke on the air. My head is spinning. I can't get up off of the floor.

It's the new technician with the long blonde ponytail that tries to help me. She had poked her head in the day room, checking up on us, gasping when she sees that I'm sprawled on the floor. She's a blur of pale blue scrubs as she hurries into the common area, hiking her pants up as she squats by my side.

She holds out her hand.

Her pale, unscarred hand.

I flinch.

To me, it's like she's shoving a poisonous snake in my face. Her skin is that dangerous.

"What are you doing down there? I know the floor can't be that comfortable. Come now, take my hand. I'll help you up."

No.

No.

The words won't come. I shake my head frantically, pulling away from her.

Her hand follows me.

No!

"No… no touching," I wheeze. The words are garbled, harsher than I mean, almost like I spit them out at her. I can't help it. "Back off."

"I'm not trying to hurt you. I just want to help."

She just wants to touch me.

"I said back off!"

This new tech slowly pulls her hand back. Her lips quirk into some semblance of a professional smile— designed to soothe me, though hell if that's gonna work right now—but it's not enough to hide the worry in her hazel eyes.

She's too new to Black Pine. She doesn't know me, though I'd bet a stack of Oreos that she's heard all about me.

That worry? It's because she has no clue what I'm

about to do. With my reputation, she's got a pretty good reason to worry.

Today, I'm good. Nothing out of the ordinary. I do what I *always* do.

I sit on my hands.

One of the other girls snickers. Whitney? Wouldn't doubt it. A high-pitched voice fills the sudden quiet next. *Zehn. Neun. Acht. Sieben…* Someone's counting backward from ten in German. That would be Allison. When she's uncomfortable, she slips into German.

It could be worse. It could be French. Allison likes to speak French when she finds something funny.

I'm so not laughing.

Dean gets up. My vision is hazy, my heart *thump-thump-thump*ing away in my chest, but I make out the big guy as he gets back to his feet and lumbers away from the couch. He squeezes himself between Martin and Casey on the other sofa.

I make sure to dodge just enough to avoid his knee bumping into my shoulder before focusing on the tech. She seems to have gotten closer to me in the last few seconds.

I don't like it.

"Riley," she says softly. So she *does* know who I am. I figured. "Listen to me. I'm sure you know that the rule's only to make sure that you guys don't touch each other. I have to touch you if I'm going to help you off the floor."

She's telling the truth. I can tell.

It doesn't matter.

"No touching," I insist.

Okay. So maybe I sound like I'm panicking a little. I *am* panicking.

No touching. It's the only rule I live by. I learned early on that bad things happen to me whenever I let someone touch me without my permission. And I'm not talking about people messing with my personal space or groping me without my consent.

I'm talking about *control*.

If you let one of the fae touch you, they can make you do things you never would—and you can't stop them. And the worst part is that it's almost impossible to tell if someone is human or not. The monsters have the power to make themselves look like anyone they want, wearing a glamour that hides who they truly are.

The fae are tricky like that. They treat humans like toys, playing with us, twisting the truth, crossing all boundaries to get permission for a touch that steals half of who you are.

Six years ago, I was blamed for the fire that killed my sister. I didn't set it—I *know* I didn't—but that didn't mean a damn thing when I finally broke down and admitted the truth about the fae. That they've followed me all my life, waiting for me to trip and offer them my hand.

Just like this tech wants me to do right now.

I made that mistake once. The golden-haired, golden-eyed fae male who convinced me that I could trust him minutes before he started the fire. Even though I knew better—I'd been coached, I'd been taught, I'd been trained better—he came so close to stealing more than a touch.

At the last second, I found the courage to tell him no, that I wouldn't follow him wherever he led. He punished me for my refusal. Me and Madelaine. I said no, she didn't, and the world as I knew it went up in flames.

My doctors spent years convincing me that the fae don't exist. Logically, I know they can't. Mythical, ethereal creatures from another world who are interested in me, a twenty-year-old orphan in the middle of nowhere? Logically, I know I created my imaginary friend, the fantastical world of Faerie, and a set of intricate rules to follow as a way to work through the abandonment issues I've dealt with since my mom disappeared when I was a baby.

The meds are supposed to help. The sessions with my therapists, my case manager, the doctors… they're supposed to help. They usually do. I can go months without feeling like I'm being watched, or worrying that the golden-eyed fae male will find me again.

And then someone tries to touch me and it all comes crashing down.

I'm not crazy. I'm not broken. I just believe in beautiful monsters who are willing to do anything they can to get their hands on me—even burn down a house with me and my sister inside of it.

The tech reaches for me.

Hell *no*.

My skin crawls as I scoot away, my back slamming

into the side of the couch. I might have gloves to protect my hands, but what about my neck, my throat, my chin? Nope. I don't know her.

I won't let her touch me.

I *can't.*

The tech hovers, hand outstretched, visibly confused. She doesn't know what to do. I almost snap at her to leave me alone, though I manage to keep my mouth shut when I see Amy step into the day room.

She's carrying a tray of drinks. Water, iced tea, juice. Some mid-morning refreshments for our downtime. Her eyebrows lift when she reads the scene. Without losing any of her usual charm, she calls out, "Is everything alright in here, Diana?"

The blonde technician rises from her crouch. "Just checking on one of the patients."

Amy's soft brown eyes land on me. Understanding dawns in an instant and she nods. While she places the tray of drinks down on an empty table, she says, "Riley, let's get up off of the floor, okay? You'll stretch your gloves out if you lay on them like that."

My gloves. Amy knows exactly what to say. I value my gloves more than anything else I own. Every Christmas Mrs. Everett buys me a new pair of gloves to cover my hands. I work so hard to soften the leather, molding them to my fingers like they're a second skin.

It's only June. Who knows if I'll get a new pair in December? I have to make these last.

Besides, I know Amy. Amy, she's safe. She gestures for Diana to back off—*finally*—giving me enough space to awkwardly climb back to my feet. It takes a few seconds for the dizziness to pass. When it does, I exhale roughly.

I feel better now.

After I wipe the palms of my dusty gloves against my pants, I slip back onto my spot on the sofa. With Dean gone, there are at least three feet separating me from Kim.

"Better?" asks Amy.

I nod.

And that's it. It's over. A peek out of the corner of my eye reveals that Diana is still looking at me curiously. Since I don't want to face her right now, I turn so that I can watch Amy take a spot next to the table where she set down the drinks. Her trusty clipboard is tucked under her arm. She pulls it out, flips the page, then clears her throat.

"In a few minutes, I'm going to let you guys come up and get some refreshments. It's Sunday, so we'll be doing some group therapy in the day room in a bit, but first I've got a quick announcement so listen up, okay? We all know that Dr. Waylon left, right?"

A couple of people vocalize their answers. I just nod. I liked Dr. Waylon. She didn't push. I was sad to see her go, though I long ago lost track of which number psychologist she was. Ninth? Tenth? Something like that.

"Good. Well, I'm happy to announce that her replacement is finally ready to take over. And, even though it's Sunday, he's decided he wants to get a jump on meeting with you guys. As the oldest group, this ward is up first."

There's a chorus of groans, me included. It's never fun when we get a new doctor because they always insist on opening up old wounds, then digging around inside of them. Even though they're all given our case files when they start at Black Pine, the doctors want to hear it straight from us. And, well, there just comes a point when I'm sick and tired of telling them that, despite all evidence otherwise, I really don't belong in here.

If they understood that the fae were real, they'd realize that everything that has ever happened to me—everything that I've ever done—is a direct reaction to *them*.

Too bad every single doctor, therapist, psychologist, whatever I've met with since I've been locked inside the asylum is convinced that my belief in the fae is one of the biggest clues that I *do* belong at Black Pine.

After a while, I just gave in and agreed with them. The fae aren't real, I've got no one to blame but myself for Madelaine's death, and my insistence that no one can touch me is an irrational phobia, not the result of being taught otherwise since I was a little girl.

Two weeks, three days, and a couple of hours.

I can do this.

As the groans die down, Amy purses her lips. She looks genuinely sorry for us. "I know, I know. But let's all be on our best behaviors, okay?" When no one answers, she sighs. "*Okay*, guys?"

I'm feeling a little grateful for the way she helped me a few minutes ago. "Right."

A couple of others half-heartedly agree with me.

Amy smiles. "That's better. Now, for those the new doctor wants to meet…"

Glancing down, she consults her clipboard. I wait for what I know is coming. I give her three names before she says mine.

"Martin."

The pyro. Makes sense.

"Whitney, you're after Martin."

Whitney might have a flair for the dramatic and a tendency to whine, but she's also been on suicide watch three separate times since she switched wards last summer. The techs keep a close eye on her. So do the doctors.

"Allison."

I hope the new doc is multilingual or good luck getting anything out of Allison. On her good days, she might humor you by speaking in English, but having her answer in French or German or even Japanese is almost as likely. I think it's really cool how she knows so many languages, too. We're only a couple of months apart in age and we've moved through the asylum together. She's not my friend, not really, but she did teach me how to say *fuck off* in like six different languages by now.

"And… Tai. The rest of you will meet with him on Monday or Tuesday."

Tai? That's… that's a surprise. Not that she calls

out Tai. I mean, his anger issues are some of the worst I've seen since I've been inside. It's just that I was almost positive she was going to call on—

"Oops. Hang on a sec. Looks like I almost forgot one."

A post-it note is stuck to the top of her page, the bright yellow square noticeable against the printed sheet. She plucks it off, bringing it closer so that she can make out the scrawl. I gulp, already resigned.

Here it comes—

"Sorry, Riley. Dr. Gillespie wants to see you first, right after we finish up here."

Yeah. Of course he does.

CHAPTER 3

In the asylum, we get a different professional every couple of weeks. Someone's always leaving or switching floors—even me. I'm used to it by now.

And, no matter what floor I'm on, every single newbie finds their way to my ward sooner or later. I absolutely hate it, but I guess I'm used to that, too. They all want to stop and gawk, probably since I've gotta be the most infamous in-patient here.

And not only because of the fatal fire.

My first memory is of the footage from the day my mother abandoned me. I never knew her, don't remember my dad, so the ten minutes of grainy, black and white video from a bank's security camera is the closest I'll ever get to the family that didn't want me.

Each second is ingrained deep in my brain. The erratic driving as she pulls into view of the camera. How she throws open her door before hopping out of an older model car. She rushes forward, talking to a patch of empty air toward the edge of the screen. It seems as if she's having an intense discussion with nobody; the camera didn't have sound so I'll never know what she said. A few minutes into it, a gas attendant appears, then leaves her alone.

It gets a little... a little *weird* after that. The footage captures her running back to the idling car, taking an infant—one-year-old Riley—from the back seat, before letting her crawl around for a few seconds in the dirt. She scoops the baby back up, gestures wildly at nobody again, then returns the baby to the car in time for the attendant to re-approach her.

I don't think she had any idea that the camera was there. Or maybe she did. Either way, she keeps her back to it most of the time as if hiding her face. Watching the footage, there are a few different angles that help me create an image of her in my mind. She was an average height, slim, with a sheet of pale hair cascading down her back. She kinda looks like me, though that might just be wishful thinking on my part. No one knows for sure that that woman was really my mom— how could they when neither one of us was ever identified?—but the older I got, the more I saw the resemblance.

Plus, the Shadow Man told me it was. Imaginary friend or not, I believed him—until he abandoned me, too.

I don't know her name. I don't know where she came from. Cops don't, either. The footage wasn't clear enough for them to figure out who she was. And no one ever came forward to report either of us missing.

The car she left behind? It had been stolen on the same day she disappeared. The only things she kept inside were me in my car seat, a half-packed diaper bag, and an iron crowbar. When I got older—when I learned the truth about the fae—I wondered if the iron was a clue that they were involved. The Shadow Man assured me that my mother was a human and, because of that, the fae weren't interested in her. But then he would never tell me why they were after me…

Still, that sucked to hear. I liked the idea that my mother had no choice but abandon me in an old, run-down gas station. I didn't want to think that she *chose* to leave me.

She did, though. Leave me, I mean. It's right there in black and white. She heads out of one frame, appearing in another as she walks away from the car. There was a side door that led to a bathroom. She goes inside. A few minutes later, the gas attendant marches over there and follows her in.

Neither one of them appears in the footage again. When the bank manager found me the next morning on her way to open up, there was no sign of my mother anywhere. The gas attendant, either.

No doubt in my mind that *he* knew about the cameras. He was extremely careful to keep his face hidden, even going so far as to wear a cap to cover it up. He was just as much a mystery, especially when the cops discovered he didn't even work there.

He *couldn't*.

The gas station closed down the year before I was born.

So whether he meant to hurt my mother or they planned it together, the undeniable truth was that two people went into that bathroom, no one left—at least, not according to the footage—and I was left to fend for myself outside of a gas station when I was barely a year old.

The papers caught wind of the story. Back then, they called me Baby Jane Doe and my picture was everywhere. Didn't help. No one came forward with any information about me. They didn't seem to know who I was, where I came from, or how two people could enter a single bathroom and disappear without a trace. I had no family, no name, no record. Neither did the woman.

I was the biggest news story in Black Pine for the rest of that summer.

Hundreds of people called in, wanting to adopt the poor, abandoned, mystery baby. The news ran nightly segments at first, then weekly, all trying to make sense out of something so damn senseless.

They never did, and eventually I became yesterday's news.

I'm what happens when the cameras turn off and the cops run out of leads. Baby Jane was a nuisance, her mother an escape artist who didn't want her kid. In the end, I got tossed into the system. I only managed to break out of it when I got put in the asylum.

It's always amazed me that my story started in that backward little town and, fifteen years later, this is where I ended up again.

My first foster family gave me a name—Riley Thorne—and a birthdate—the day I came to live with them. They were a nice couple and they tried their best to shield me from the truth of it all. I don't blame them for trying. Or giving me up five years later when it became clear that I wasn't like other little girls.

Name stuck, though. That's something, at least.

I've always liked Riley better than Jane, anyway.

DOCTOR GILLESPIE IS NOT WHAT I'M expecting.

He's younger than I thought he'd be, for one thing. Thirty, maybe thirty-five. A babyface. White guy with pasty skin. His short hair is a brassy red that clashes with the green and gold plaid button-down shirt he's got on. Bright blue eyes shine from behind a pair of gold-rimmed glasses. He even has a small goatee covering a pretty weak-looking chin.

He stands up and comes around his desk to meet me, holding out his hand.

I don't take it.

"Ah… that's right." His voice is nasal, like he has a cold or something. "I remember that from your file. The haphephobia."

My hands clench inside of my gloves. I *hate* that word.

"I don't like to be touched," I tell him, not bothering to hide my scowl. "That doesn't mean I'm afraid of it."

"Let's call it a poor choice of words on my part then, shall we?" Getting the hint, Dr. Gillespie pulls his arm back, folds his fingers into a fist, absently rubs the side of his pressed khakis, then gestures for me to step into his office. "Come on in, Riley. Take a seat."

I have half a mind to pretend that I'm not Riley. Something else I hate? How all of the doctors and the techs act like they know everything about me when they wouldn't even be able to pick me out of a line-up unless someone else pointed out who I was beforehand. Just because I'm the first patient Amy sent to see him, that doesn't automatically make me Riley Thorne.

And that's when I remember the whole haphephobia exchange. Yeah, I totally gave my identity away when I refused to shake his hand. Plus, the leather gloves stretching past my wrists are probably a pretty big clue, too.

He's got me.

Annoyed, I ask, "Where?"

"Excuse me?"

I wave at the three seats haphazardly positioned in front of his cluttered desk. Every flat surface in the room is completely covered: mountains of books, folders, reams of paper, half-packed moving boxes. It looks like a bomb went off in here.

This used to be Dr. Waylon's office. Before that, Dr. Froud. Dr. Calvin, too. Dr. McNeil. None of the real big doctors—the ones who have convinced themselves they can fix… no *rehabilitate* us wayward juveniles—seem to stick around Black Pine for long. I swear, it's like every time I'm finally getting used to one, it's time for them to leave. And then the next shrink wonders why my abandonment issues never get any better.

I've lost track of how many people have occupied this corner office. Each one left their stamp while they used it, but it was always clear it belonged to a medical professional. This disaster? You could've fooled me. This is definitely the messiest it's ever been. Boxes are stacked everywhere, all in different stages of being unpacked. One of his diplomas is hanging crookedly behind the crowded desk. The desktop is covered with manila patient files.

Dr. Gillespie's cheeks turn the same color as his hair. Mumbling an apology under his breath, he swoops down and clears the seat closest to me. His arms full, he turns in a circle before moving his pile next to the filing cabinet by the window.

"Don't mind the mess," he says with an awkward laugh. "The facility director thought I was going to start tomorrow, but I wanted to do an informal session with a few of you juveniles since I arrived a couple of days early. I had hoped to be moved in before they started but I guess we'll both have to make do."

Once his arms are free again, he motions for me to take my seat. I do, perching my gloved hands royally on the arms of the chairs as soon as Dr. Gillespie slumps into his seat behind his desk. My back is straight, my gaze locked on the nervous doctor. I don't break eye contact, purposely watching him the way a cat would watch a mouse.

I think I'm making him uncomfortable. His face is now the color of a firetruck.

Good.

He's the one who wanted this session. He wanted to see what Riley Thorne was made of. And, except for how vulnerable I get during my panic attacks, I'm made of stronger stuff than any of my doctors ever expect.

Okay, then.

Let's go.

Clearing his throat, squirming a bit under my direct stare, Dr. Gillespie attempts to regain control of our meeting. He flips open a notepad and picks up a pen, tip to the paper, ready to write down anything he finds interesting.

Not if I can help it.

"Now, Riley," he says, "how are you feeling today?"

Standard question. I have to answer it at least five times a day from five different people.

I give him my standard response. "Feel fine."

"How's your mood?"

I shrug. "Okay, I guess."

"That's good."

I don't have any idea how he can make sense of his mess, but he does. Picking one manila folder out from a stack of ten, he opens it up and begins to rifle through all of the papers inside. The stack is at least half an inch thick.

I can only imagine what my other doctors have written about me on those sheets.

Dr. Gillespie grabs his pen, scribbles something on a middle page, then closes the whole folder. He rests his hands on top of it. "I'll be honest. I'm sure you know that I've already gone over your file. Still, I'd rather hear it from you. Tell me, Riley. Why are you at Black Pine?"

My jaw goes tight.

Why am I at Black Pine? It's bad enough that I'm forced to admit the reasons why I'm here every morning during community group. Why does he need me to say it? He has the answer at his fingertips.

My first instinct is to snap that I'm a wayward juvenile. Black Pine's full name is a bit of a joke inside, especially among the older crowd. What the hell is that supposed to mean? Wayward juvenile? I guess it's better than saying it's a psych ward for kiddies, right?

And they wonder why we all just call it the asylum.

I don't say that, though. Instead, I fiddle with the edge of my glove, pulling on it, stretching out the leather. Under my breath, I mutter, "I'll give you a hint. It's not haphephobia."

He hears me.

"Fair enough."

Okay. His easy comment catches me off-guard. With Dr. Froud, a flippant comment like that would have earned me a ten-minute lecture on respect. Respecting him, respecting me, respecting the facility, respecting my diagnosis.

He was a bore, let me tell you. I was glad when Dr. Waylon finally replaced him.

Dr. Gillespie's glasses slide down his narrow nose as he looks over at me. He shoves them up, but not before I can see the earnest look in his eyes. Oh, man. He's one of *those*. The type of doctor who thinks we can be friends, who thinks that he'll finally be the one to make me all better.

Wonderful.

"I'm curious about the gloves, though," he says. "You want to tell me the story behind them?"

Do I want to?

No.

Do I know better than to push my luck with a new doctor?

Yup.

For one second, I think about taking my gloves off to make a bigger impact, then decide against it. I can barely stomach the blotches, the scars, the ruined skin myself—and they're *my* hands. I really don't like anyone else to see them. Dr. Gillespie is no exception.

Glancing down, I move my hands into my lap, running one hand over the other, grateful for the leather that protects them and hides them at the same time.

"I got burned really bad a couple of years ago," I explain. He's read my file. He knows exactly how I got burned, too. "I had to have skin grafts. When my hands finally healed, the doctors said I could keep gloves on if they felt too sensitive."

"That was in the accident," he guesses. "When your foster sister died."

That's how everyone here refers to it. The *accident*. It's better than what the courts called it.

The murder.

"Yeah," I admit, finally looking away from him. My last glimpse is of his impish face and the satisfied smile he wears.

It isn't a game, even if I treat my stay in Black Pine like that half the time. It makes the endless routine—the tiring monotony—more manageable when I do. But it isn't a game. Not really.

Even so, at that moment, we both know that Dr. Gillespie has won this round.

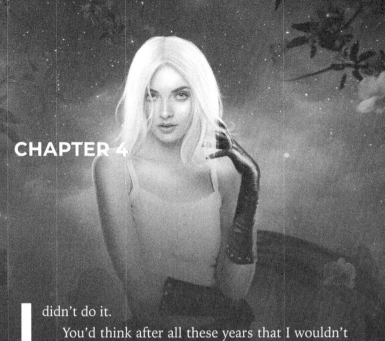

CHAPTER 4

I didn't do it.

You'd think after all these years that I wouldn't have to remind myself of the truth. As I step aside to let Martin enter Dr. Gillespie's office, my heart is thudding, my stomach tight. I didn't do it, but it's super hard to convince anyone of your innocence when you're an in-patient in a facility like Black Pine.

After a while, you give up on trying. Either the doctors believe you or they don't. Whatever. The only important thing is that *you* don't forget.

I didn't kill Madelaine. I couldn't. We might not have been blood, but we were still sisters. I never would've hurt her. My hands are destroyed because I tried to *save* her.

Despite what the papers first reported, the courts didn't really think I had anything to do with her death. If I did? It wasn't on purpose. During the autopsy, the medical examiner discovered that Madelaine had a broken neck. At fifteen, I was barely one-ten. I couldn't even open a pickle jar without Mr. Everett's help. No way I could have done that to her on my own.

But the fire...

The fire is what made the cops, then the courts look at me like a suspect. And that's because I told them that it was a beautiful man—no, a beautiful *fae*—with long gold-colored hair and glowing golden eyes who started the fire *and* killed my sister.

He was the one who tricked Madelaine, charming her toward him, enticing her to give him her neck only for him to snap it easily. He's the one who built a circle around her body and set it on fire. The one who dared me to come and get her, who laughed as my hands burned.

He did it all. And then, my hands blistered, my throat raw from screaming, he vanished and I was left to take all the blame.

Kindly at first, then more firmly, everybody told me that I made him up. That he couldn't possibly exist— that the fae didn't exist—and I used this fantasy to explain the fire. The official statement was that I had a breakdown when I found that Madelaine had died in such a tragic accident. In my grief, I lit a fire as if I was trying to make it all go away.

Of course, then I went ahead and told them about Nine. I spoke about my Shadow Man in such great detail that they decided that my troubles started long before I was fifteen. I just didn't get a diagnosis until then.

Schizophrenia at first, until they settled on schizo-typal personality disorder once I told them that, while I see and talk to the fae, I understand they're not *real*.

Anxiety with near-catatonic panic attacks.

And, no matter what I told Dr. Gillespie, just a touch of haphephobia.

That is why I'm here.

It's been a long six years. I learned early on that no one else believes in the fae so I started to pretend that I didn't, either. After a while, I wasn't pretending. So long as I take my morning meds, I'm fine. Sure, I lose it when I think someone might touch me, but that's just self-preservation. Better safe than sorry, right? Nine warned me not to let anyone touch me. So what if there's no Nine? That means the warning came from my own mind and, if there's one person in this world I can rely on, it's me.

I'm the only one who has never let me down.

As I head back toward the day room, my hands folded, gloved palm pressing against gloved palm, I let my thoughts return to Dr. Gillespie. Young guy, eager to prove himself.

I give him six weeks.

Art therapy is underway by the time I rejoin my group.

Because we need more space to get creative, we don't have art therapy in any of the smaller group rooms. We take over the day room, spreading out on the sofas and the chairs, using plastic tray tables and the kind of art supplies you see in pre-schools.

I'm gonna be twenty-one, and I still spend my weekends drawing with crayon.

Lucky, lucky me.

When I was younger, back when I was grouped in on some of the other floors, it was a little different. Black Pine has a program that works with the true juveniles, putting them through school, helping us prepare for real life when we're finally released. I got my GED by the time I was seventeen, and I went through all the prep courses. I know how to balance a checkbook, use a program to fill out my taxes, and I've even done mock interviews to prepare me for getting a job. When they let me out, I should be fine on my own.

There are more prep courses when you get moved to the final ward. Our group—nineteen through twenty-one—is all about getting prepared for release. One way or another, you age out of Black Pine at twenty-one. With a good report, they put you into a halfway house, help you transition on the outside. A bad one means moving on to another facility.

Yeah. No, thanks.

Like sessions and meetings with our counselors and social workers, those courses are scheduled on weekdays only. Weekends are considered downtime. Art therapy is a definite, just like extra television time if our ward's been good.

Because it's technically considered a group session,

the television is off. With everyone hard at work, all I can hear is the muffled rubbing of crayons against paper, Dean's occasional muttering, and the therapist's constant stream of half-hearted encouragement.

After what happened this morning, I make sure to take one of the few open seats by the closed window. Water streams down the frosted glass; it's still raining hard out there. The therapist—a slender Asian man with short black hair and a kind smile—brings me a tray table, a few sheets of paper, and a handful of crayons.

He's been here before and he knows better. Instead of handing the supplies to me, he places them on an empty seat not too far from where I'm sitting.

"Thanks."

"We just started, Riley. Today's session is an easy one. I want you to draw something that's been on your mind lately. Turn your paper over when you're done, then we'll discuss your feelings at the close of today's session." He nods when I reach out, grabbing the tray table, slapping my hand on top of the crayons so that they don't roll right off. "Any questions before you begin?"

I shake my head. This is pretty common for art therapy. I know what to do.

Same rules as normal. Nothing morbid or gory. Nothing violent. Nothing that gives away the truth that some of us are kinda disturbed. Art therapy is supposed to be productive, yet positive.

We save our demons for the psychologists.

My drawing is a repeat, too. Choosing a grey crayon over white paper, I begin to draw the stone angel that watches over Madelaine's grave. She's never too far from my thoughts but, since my dream last night, she's been constantly on my mind. The meeting with Dr. Gillespie didn't help me even a little.

I don't plan on doing the whole end-of-session sharing time, though. No point. Most of the other patients have seen this same drawing before. Even if I refuse to talk about my sister, they all know what the stone angel means.

Oh, well. I gave up trying to convince them of the truth, too. Either they think I'm responsible for her death or they simply don't give a crap. It's not like it's their business, anyway.

I'm just adding the small chip that marks the stone angel's right wing when the quiet is broken up by the sound of someone crying. And not just *cry*, with sniffles and whimpers and barely-there tears. Nope. These are *sobs*. Big, wet, wracking sobs that start as a groan and end with a choking gasp for air.

My crayon slips from my hand. Like everyone else in the room, my head shoots up, searching for the sobber. I feel a twinge deep in my gut. I recognize it. It sounds like someone is in the middle of a panic attack—except, for once, it isn't me.

It's Carolina, the girl from the meds line this morning.

She's not too far from me, sitting on one of the sofas. Her tray table was perched on her lap. As I watch her sob, her body shakes and the table somehow falls. I could almost swear I saw her shove it away from her the instant before it dropped but, honestly, I'm not even thinking about that since the tray table bounces and her artwork flutters and lands a few inches away from my feet.

Not gonna lie. Since it's Carolina, I'm expecting to see like a mirror or a supermodel or something like that drawn on her paper. I remember, last time the therapist told us to draw up something that we wished for, she drew a plate of food.

I'm not wrong. In the center of the page, Carolina used the black crayon to draw a very tall, very skinny figure with long hair. Two dots—grey—must be her eyes. A red blob is attached to the figure's hand. An apple? Maybe. It does have a thin brown line drawn on the top, almost like a stem.

I don't know why the drawing would set her off. It seems innocent enough to me. But the rest of the paper is blank and Carolina is still crying.

The therapist rushes over, swooping the paper off of the floor as if he also figures this drawing is the reason behind her outburst. Folding it into quarters, he hides it from sight before settling next to Carolina, talking softly, trying to calm her down.

Good luck.

It's pointless. The entire group gives up on their drawings, watching as Carolina dissolves further into inconsolable sobs; I know I'm not alone in being glad it's not me who's lost it this time. I'll give the therapist credit, too. He tries his best to get her to explain her reaction but, in the end, he gestures for one of the techs to take over.

Louis retrieves Carolina, ushering her out of the day room and down the hall. We all listen as her sobs die down, not because she's gotten over it, but because she's gone far enough away to keep being an interruption.

Too late for that.

By the time she's gone and the art therapist has regained control over our group, the hour is up. I'm kinda glad.

Even though I'm not quite done with my picture yet, I turn the paper over so that I don't have to look at Madelaine's angel.

WE'RE SUPPOSED TO GET OUR NIGHTTIME meds from the nursing station. Not me. I've always been one of the only exceptions.

That night, after dinner, I don't go back to the day room with the other kids. Back when I first came to live at Black Pine, I used to have this really weird habit of sitting in the corner and talking to the shadows that played out on the wall before they got my meds regulated. Now, just in case, I get more quiet time than most.

I blame Dr. McNeil. Smartass. He's the one who decided it would be better if I went straight to my room at night where, if I start to talk to the walls again, at least I don't rile up the other kids.

Amy's my morning tech; her shift is over at six. The earliest I go back to my room is seven so that means I have to deal with a nighttime tech. Of course, they don't trust a tech to bring the meds to our rooms. Duncan, my regular nighttime tech, makes sure to accompany whichever nurse is on duty. She brings the meds, while the big goon stands guard, making sure that I behave and take my pills.

Tonight's nurse is Nurse Stanley.

Nurse Stanley is a sour-faced woman in her early fifties who is nearly as thin as Carolina. She has a perpetual frown and hands that look like claws. Her bleached-blonde hair is pulled back so tight that her eyes seem to bulge out of her head. She reminds me of a frog that's been starved for too long.

She even sounds like she's croaking when she says it's time for my meds. I can smell the smoke that clings to her uniform. At least that explains the croaking— though I still like my version better.

Duncan looms in my doorway, his back to the hall, massive arms slapped across his wide chest. He's so tall and bulky, he barely fits. I resist the urge to roll my eyes. The way he stares me down is overkill. I'm probably the least likely escape risk in the entire ward, yet he always insists on watching me like I am.

Nurse Stanley carries a small plastic tray with two dixie cups on it, just like normal. She holds out one of the cups, pinching the bottom with two fingers, and says, "Three pills tonight, Thorne. Two white and a pink. Dr. Gillespie put the order in himself."

Nurse Stanley is used to my haphephobia. There's no chance of an accidental touch when she leaves the top of the cup free for me to grab.

Taking the cup from her, I peek inside. She's right. I poke the little pink one with the tip of my glove. It's new—and that's different. I haven't had a med change since they took my blue pill away.

That one wasn't so bad. Whenever I saved a couple to take at once, they made me feel like I was floating on a cloud.

I wonder what the pink pill will do before realizing it doesn't matter. I don't plan on taking it tonight.

Before Nurse Stanley starts to get impatient, I toss the contents of the cup in my mouth. Practice makes it easy to stick the two white pills behind my upper molars. The pink pill is so small I nearly swallow it. I manage to slip it underneath my tongue just in time.

I drink the water from the second cup carefully. As the tablets melt, the taste is really awful, but I don't give it away on my face. Once I've drunken enough, I make sure to open my mouth and show Nurse Stanley that my meds are gone.

She grunts and takes my water cup back. "Lights out at ten, Thorne."

I give her a tight-lipped smile and wait for her to leave. I've suspected for a while that she knows I don't always take my nighttime meds—too bad she can't prove it. Honestly, I'm not so sure that she'd give a crap either way. And it's not like I do it all the time. Only when it's Nurse Stanley, and even then so occasionally that she hasn't had the chance to catch me at it yet.

It's just... I can't stand how my sleeping pills make me feel. I don't dream when I'm doped up, and they leave me feeling hazy, lost, and stupid when I wake up the next morning. So what if I miss a dose or two? At least I take my morning meds religiously.

I'm not so stupid that I spit the pills out right away. Sometimes Nurse Stanley comes back or she might send Duncan in to see if I need anything before they lock me in for the night. I count to fifty before I figure the coast is clear.

I pluck the three pills from their hiding places and stash them in the toe of my slipper with the rest of my supply.

And if the bottom of the slipper is crusted with dried, caked-on mud? I pretend not to notice before tucking my slipper under my bed again.

CHAPTER 5

I'm just falling asleep when I hear it. My name. Whispered as softly as a breeze drifting through the night's sky, I swear I hear someone say my name.

"Riley."

My door is locked. I have no phone. No radio. No television. The walls are so thick, there's not even an echo whenever Emma screams at night and, on her bad days, she has some awful dreams.

I shouldn't be able to hear a damn thing—

"Riley."

—and then I hear it again.

I almost stop breathing. It catches in my throat, my heart starting to race so fast—beat so loud—that it almost drowns out the inexplicable whisper. Inside my gloves, my hands grow clammy, slick with a sudden sweat. There's no way I should have heard that, I'd only be proving everyone in Black Pine right if I admit that I did, but I can't... I can't *deny* it.

That voice? The one I shouldn't be hearing?

It's eerily familiar, a voice I know all too well.

Even if I haven't heard him call my name in almost forever.

"Riley..."

It's a mistake to open my eyes. The room is dark; I can barely make out anything. A weak stream of light fills the gap between my door and the floor. Between that and the faint, hazy moonlight breaking through the almost purple cloud cover, inky, black shadows bounce off of the end of my bed. Anyone could be hiding in my room and hell if I'd know. I'm as good as blind and, suddenly, I wish I hadn't realized that.

I squint. "Hello?"

My voice comes out strangled. Unsure. A second later, I'm not positive I said a word at all.

Nobody answers. *He* certainly doesn't.

I pull my thin blanket up, kissing my chin while keeping my eyes narrowed at the darkness. My attention is yanked toward the far corner of my room. Where the two walls meet, the shadows are deeper than they should be. It's not just dark there—it's pitch black.

And that's when I see it.

Call it my overactive imagination, wishful thinking, or a trick of the shadows. Whatever it is, I'm still staring when I catch a flash of silver from the dark depths. Silver—

The Shadow Man had eyes of silver.

That's it. I'm not going through this shit again. Gulping, I close my eyes so tightly that I create bright sparks dancing across the inside of my eyelids. My heart skips a beat, my fingers trembling as I slip my left hand over the edge of the bed. I lean over, searching the floor.

Where is it? Where— *there*.

My slipper is right where I left it.

Desperate times call for desperate measures. I don't even care which ones I grab. Scooping a couple of pills from my stash, I fumble in my self-imposed darkness, managing to toss them into my mouth after a few false starts.

With the memory of that silver flash fresh in my mind, I swallow the pills dry.

Anything to go to sleep right now.

"Tell me about Madeline, Riley."

At Dr. Gillespie's opening comment, I stiffen.

He's just going straight for it, isn't he?

Normally, I would brush him off. Every single one of my doctors, my psychiatrists, my counselors, and my psychologists learn before long that there are two topics that guarantee I'm gonna clam up: my mom and Madelaine.

Thing is, I'm still kinda shaky from last night, from the voice I shouldn't have heard and the wave of fear that hasn't quite subsided yet, so when Dr. Gillespie mentions Madelaine so easily, all I can mutter is, "You're saying it wrong. Her name was Madelaine. And there's nothing more to tell."

Dr. Gillespie nods, then makes a note on the upgraded journal lying flat on his desktop.

It's Monday. I have a session with Dr. Waylon first thing on Mondays and, now that she's gone, I get to spend the hour with Dr. Gillespie instead. My routine at Black Pine is simple enough: three sessions a week with my psychologist, and daily check-ins with any of the available psychotherapists. As annoying as it was, yesterday's meeting with Dr. Gillespie counted as a check-in.

This is my first real session. He wasted no time at all before asking about Madelaine. That's better than talking about my diagnosis, I guess. Considering my dreamless sleep and my sinking suspicion that my auditory hallucinations might have started up again, it's safer to keep the discussion centered on Madelaine.

Of course, I'm not about to offer up any information myself. Everything he needs to know about my sister or me is in my file. If he wants more, he's going to have to drag it out of me.

Something's different about the doctor today. Despite how heavy my head feels, how the whole world seems fuzzy and hazy to me, I immediately picked up on the change. Maybe it's because of his office. It's in a much better state. The desk is orderly, clean and organized, and the few boxes that aren't unpacked yet are stacked neatly in one corner.

Dr. Gillespie's definitely more prepared this session. Glancing at something written in his portfolio, he peers at me through his glasses while wearing a determined expression. "Let's start at the beginning. How long did you know her? She was the Everetts' first adopted daughter. Isn't that right?"

"Yup."

"And you were there for three years?"

"Two."

"So you knew Madeline—Made*laine*, sorry… you knew her for two years?"

I nod. No harm in admitting that. "Sounds about right."

"And you got along well with her?"

"Best of friends."

Dr. Gillespie raises his eyebrows, obviously intrigued by—or concerned with—my flippant attitude. I'm too tired to care. Plus, I've got way too much running through my mind to worry about pissing off the new guy. Jutting my chin at him, I dare him to keep asking me questions that I have no intention of really answering.

He purses his lips. "It's been six years since the accident. Do you miss her?"

Every single day. "Yes."

"Mmm. Are you sad that she's gone?"

"Of course I am."

He nods, picks up his pen. "Do you wish it was you

instead? The one who died in the accident… do you wish it was you?"

Wow. He really went there, didn't he? With a snort, I turn my head. I'm not even gonna try to give him a half-assed answer to *that* one. It's a trick question. I say no and I have no remorse. I say yes and they put me on a watch. No, thanks.

But then he tosses out a question that has my head jerking so quickly, I nearly give myself whiplash—

"Why did you let her die?"

It's the *let* that cuts me to the bone.

It's one thing to accuse me of doing any of it. Setting the fire, making her fall—because that's how they explain away her broken neck. She was found in the basement of the empty house so, obviously, she fell and snapped her own neck. The accusations are nothing but background noise to me by now because I *know* I didn't do it.

That doesn't mean I'm not responsible. I am. If I hadn't let the fae male touch my hand, Madelaine would still be alive and there's nothing I can do to change that now.

And somehow this doctor I've known for like five minutes has picked up on it.

I'm on my feet before I realize how much his pointed question affected me. I thought I could do this. Meeting with another psychologist fresh to Black Pine… I thought I could do this like I've done a dozen times before. Nope. And maybe he's better than I thought. Maybe he did it on purpose, a shot in the dark that managed to hit home. I don't know.

But this is why I refuse to talk about my sister if I can get away with it.

My fingers flex. I need to feel leather wrapping my fingers, my palms, my wrists… I need the reassurance it gives me as my hands start to tremble and shake. I slap my palms against my sides, my gloves muffling the sound of the hit as I try to hide my reaction.

Yeah. That's easier said than done.

Dr. Gillespie's lips curve just enough to show how pleased he is at my reaction. Torn between anger, regret, and shame, I glare over at him. His eyes shine behind his glasses.

I want to smack that smug expression off of his face.

"What kind of question is that?" I snap back. "What kind of doctor would even *ask* something like that?"

In an instant, I know I've gone too far. Dr. Gillespie might be new, and he might be young, but he's a professional employed by the facility that runs my life. He's the one with the power.

And he knows it.

His whole face closes off as he points at my vacant seat. "Sit down, Riley."

I don't move.

The doctor raps his pen lightly against the top of his desk. "There's still plenty of today's session to go. Don't make me tell you to take your seat again."

His nasal voice goes sharp, straight to the point.

There's a threat in there that he doesn't bother to hide, slowly reaching his hand out toward the old-fashioned handset phone perched on the right corner of his desk. With the press of one button, he could alert anyone in the asylum that I'm acting out.

I know exactly what will happen if I refuse to sit and he hits that button.

I have to listen. Last time I openly disobeyed one of the head doctors, they confined me to my room for three days with only my own distorted memories to distract me. They messed with my meds then, too. I got maybe six hours of sleep the entire time. I was a mess by the end of that suspension, though I can say I definitely learned my lesson.

So did my doctors. I got my blue pills back for that entire summer.

I sit down, though I'm not happy about it. Crossing my arms over my chest, I clamp down on my teeth so hard that it sends a shock of pain along my jaw. I fight to hide my wince. Dr. Gillespie sees it anyway.

Behind his gold-rimmed glasses, he sees everything.

To my surprise, his voice gentles as he says, "You made your point. You don't want to focus on Madelaine today? That's fine. I understand that. We have plenty of sessions ahead of us. We can table her for another time. Would you like that?"

So maybe he's being a little condescending. Whatever.

"Yeah." I force myself to relax, to let it go before the anger overwhelms me and my emotions take over. I'm still not over yesterday's panic attack, either, and that's clear. I shudder on a breath, making myself small as I lean back into my chair. I'll regroup in a second, ready myself for round two in a bit. Just... just not yet. I shake my head. "Yeah, I would."

"Okay. We can do that. I want you to know that I'm just here to help you, Riley."

Ugh. Now he sounds earnest.

Was I overreacting?

Possibly.

With a shrug, I tell him, "I know."

"Your sister is a delicate subject."

Yeah, that's putting it mildly. "Mm-hmm."

"What about Nine?"

And, just like that, any gratitude I worked up because he was willing to drop Madelaine vanishes at that one syllable. Because Nine? It's not just a number. Not to me.

It's a man.

The *Shadow Man*.

I blink, try to come up with a way to change the subject, then decide my best bet is to play dumb.

"Nine what?"

"Not what," corrects the doctor. "Who."

"I don't know what you're talking about."

"That was his name, wasn't it? Your... childhood friend?"

Is he serious? Good god. He's trying to be *delicate*.

I guess there's no point in pretending now. "Oh. Are

you asking me about my first documented hallucination, Dr. Gillespie?"

Hallucination. That's how all of the adults in charge refer to him now. When I was a kid, my foster parents called Nine my imaginary friend. When I was old enough to know better, he became a hallucination.

To me, Nine was always just the Shadow Man.

My earliest memories involve Nine. Without a family of my own, he became the one constant in my life. He followed me from foster home to foster home, almost as if he could track me anywhere. He didn't always come to see me, though. Nine had his own life, his own responsibilities, and he could go weeks at a time between his sporadic visits. But when he did appear? It was as if no time had passed at all.

I don't know why I loved him so much. He was cold and he was distant. Firm. He had no patience for my tantrums, and he threatened to not come back whenever I begged for him to stay. That was just Nine, though. In his own way, he showed me how dedicated he was to me. Only visiting at night when the shadows came, vanishing long before the sun rose the next morning, he spent years teaching me, coaching me, taking care of me in the guarded way he had.

No mom. No dad. Nine was the only one I could count on until I made it to the Everetts and I bonded with Madelaine.

I don't want to talk about my sister. But Nine?

I can talk about Nine.

Before Black Pine, that would've been impossible.

I mean it. Before I came to the asylum, I was so twisted up inside. I was convinced that the Shadow Man who visited me my entire childhood had to be kept a secret. Nine insisted on it. He warned me that, if I told anyone about him, there would be consequences.

I was a kid. What did I know?

So I blabbed, and he disappeared. I haven't seen him since I got tossed inside of Black Pine.

The doctors told me it was because they finally got my medications regulated. For the longest time, I was convinced it was because I spilled all of Nine's secrets at my hearing. Then I eventually accepted that he was just a figment of my imagination and I was glad that I banished him from my brain.

At least, I *thought* that he was gone for good. For the last six years, I worked with my psychotherapists, my techs, my mental health counselors, and my social worker to accept that Nine was nothing more than a figure in my mind.

So why did I hear his voice again last night?

No. Not going there.

Didn't hear a voice.

Nope.

Okay. Dr. Gillespie wants to talk about Nine? Sure. Fine. I'll talk about him. Maybe that will send the Shadow Man away again.

Two weeks, two days now, and a couple of hours before I'm out of the asylum. This is not the time to imagine that Nine's back.

I rub my forehead, pushing my bangs out of my face. "What do you want to know about him?"

"Everything you can tell me. From the beginning. How far back can you remember him being around? What's your first memory of him?"

That's... that's an unusual approach. Most of my doctors feel like they have to convince me over and over again that Nine was never real. After a while, it sunk in—rational thinking tells me that there's no such thing as magic and the fae and an otherworld called Faerie where anything can happen.

Still, even all these years later, sometimes I ask myself: *what if*? What if it was all real? Nine and his shadows, and the golden-eyed fae with the power to control fire?

Is Dr. Gillespie doing the same thing? Seems like it. Who knows? Maybe this is some new form of therapy, humoring the patient, actually believing that their hallucinations and their delusions are true.

I decide to go for it.

"I was very tiny, three or four, or maybe even younger. I'm not sure—it's like he's always been there. He always came and sat with me in the nursery at the Thorne's house, singing strange songs to help me fall asleep." I don't mention that the songs weren't in any language I've heard since then, or that I would stay up and listen because having him near made me feel safe. "He didn't come every night. Didn't expect him to. Busy guy, but he always said someone sent him to watch over me."

I almost add that, when I was little, I used to think he meant my mom. I don't anymore. Like forgetting the threat of the fae, I long ago accepted that my mom never wanted me.

"Really?" He sounds surprised. "Three or four? That soon? And you remember it?"

And… we're back to my diagnosis again.

None of the professionals can believe that my symptoms manifested so early—or that it took until I was fifteen and Madelaine was dead before anyone took them seriously.

I clench my fists so tightly that my fingers are straining against my gloves, pulling the leather taut. "You'd be surprised at how far back my memory goes."

"What did he look like? Did he change his appearance over time or look the same?"

That's a pretty standard question. And a safe one.

"They can make themselves look however they want." Dr. Gillespie wags his pen at me, gesturing for me to elaborate. I shrug. "Black hair. He used to wear it short, then let it grow out some. Crazy silver eyes, like dimes or something shining out of his face. He was super pale, too." He was also the prettiest man I've ever seen in my life, but I don't tell the doctor that. Instead, grasping for something else to say, I add, "He looks exactly the opposite of the golden fae."

I regret the words almost as soon as they're out.

His hand twitches. The pen he was clutching slips from between his suddenly lax fingers. "Fae?"

Oops. My throat goes dry, the memory of that fae

trying to push it's way through. I'll talk about Nine. But the monster? "I... I don't want to talk about that. Forget I said anything."

Dr. Gillespie is wearing that same knowing look from before. He's read my file. There's no way he doesn't know about the golden fae, a creature of fire and laughter and the power to make others do whatever he wants them to. Like how he lured Madelaine to him, or how he caused me to wear these gloves forever.

Nine is safe. I'm not afraid of him.

But the golden fae who promised to come after me?

I visibly shake.

Dr. Gillespie sees that, too. Aware that I'm so close to the edge, he backs off. "Then tell me more about Nine." When I don't argue, he pushes. "So your first memory is from very early on. What about your last? How often did he appear to you? What would he say?"

As someone who was initially diagnosed as schizophrenic before my personality disorder was pinpointed, these are the sorts of questions that I'm used to. I'm so relieved that he's letting the golden fae go without pressing me for answers, I willingly continue to discuss Nine.

Besides, I know what he's expecting from me. He wants crazy? I'll give him bonkers.

For the next twenty minutes I ramble on, telling the doctor everything I remember about Nine: from how he rarely strayed from the shadows, to the very clear warnings he gave about never letting anyone touch me. I probably just confirmed my haphephobia to Dr. Gillespie. That's fine. Like I told him before, I'm not afraid to be touched—not exactly. It's more like I was brainwashed from a very early age that if you let anyone with Faerie blood touch you, you give them power over you. A touch of your hand is like giving the fae permission to reach inside of you and steal part of your soul. For the magical race, that power is everything.

Madelaine's murderer proved that six years ago.

Logically, I know the fae can't exist. Deep down, I accept that they do—and that no one else will ever believe me. So I might as well keep on pretending.

It's a good thing it doesn't bother me when I lie—to the doctors, the techs, or even myself—or my stomach would always be tied up in knots.

There's a strange look on Dr. Gillespie's face as I speak. His pen is still where he dropped it. I don't think he took a single note. He's peering at me closely, as if trying to figure out if I really believe any of what I just told him.

This is new to me, too. For once, I told one of my doctors the absolute truth, even if I stopped short of admitting that I heard Nine's voice for the first time in years last night. Let him think I'm lying. It's freeing to realize that I honestly don't give a crap what this man thinks of me.

I'm out in two weeks, two days, and a couple of hours. My release is already in motion. Unless I do something really terrible, I'm out in half a month.

When I'm done—when there's nothing left I want to share about the Shadow Man—Dr. Gillespie takes a deep breath. I don't think he knows what to make of any of that. We both gotta know that my file says I'm not a big talker mainly 'cause I have a hard time connecting to other people.

But that wasn't for Dr. Gillespie. That was all for me.

He waits another few seconds before he chuckles weakly. "Quite... quite an imaginative child."

"Yeah." I shouldn't feel this triumphant. "That's what each of my first four foster families said, too."

And the point goes to Riley this time around.

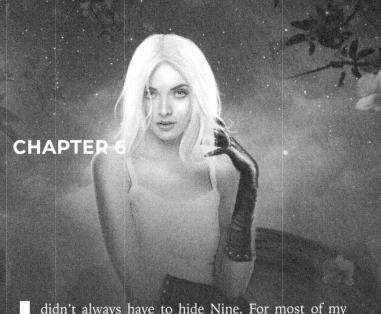

CHAPTER 6

I didn't always have to hide Nine. For most of my life, though, I did.

When I was little, barely a toddler, my first foster family—the Thornes—thought it was cute. Nine was the opposite of a bogeyman, someone who came to protect me instead of scaring the shit out of me. He told me stories, but he made a mistake in trusting that I would keep them to myself. Five-year-olds don't know how to keep secrets. And the Thornes didn't know what to do with a child who preferred the company of shadows.

I moved in with the Baxters next. He was... he was careful. When he found me—and he always found me—Nine made sure to come late at night, long after my new foster parents were asleep. I was so happy to see him again that I was willing to promise him anything. I kept him a secret for two years while he spent count-

less nights telling me about his home—about Faerie—
and the race of people who lived there.

The Blessed Ones and the Cursed Ones. Despite the
names, he warned me that neither of the fae were good
—or to be trusted. And, most important of all, I should
never, ever give one of them permission to touch me.

I was a kid. I didn't know better. Nine was my
whole world. He told me how the fae could use glamour, one of their special magic tricks, and make it so
they looked like a regular human. How was I supposed
to know a real person from the bogeymen he put in my
head?

I didn't.

I had my first full-blown panic attack in first grade
when the gym teacher grabbed my arm and I wasn't
expecting it. Shit hit the fan back then. In the end, the
teacher was suspended, the Baxters couldn't handle
my new condition, and they put me back in the
system.

So then I got shipped off to the Morrisons.

They were a married couple of fiction writers. A
little bit hippie-dippy, they both encouraged my imagination and even understood my pre-teen need for
space.

Well, in the beginning they did.

I trusted them. I hoped they would be able to
protect me from the fae during the day the same way
that Nine did at night. Yeah, *no*. Not really. When I
admitted there was a Shadow Man who visited me
while they slept, telling me stories of Faerie and the

fae, my foster parents thought I was a creative just like them.

When they found me hiding under my bed, looking for comfort in the shadows there, all because I swore that the neighbor's dog had eyes of fire and I was terrified it might be a fae in disguise, they started to get a little worried.

When I screamed bloody murder one night after Mr. Morrison tried to tuck me in, they decided I might just have too vivid of an imagination for them.

Nine followed me to the Wilsons, too. I was about twelve then. Older. More wary. I started to ask him questions—mostly about why he kept visiting me, but I tried to learn more about my mom, too—and never really got any answers from him. My hero worship was starting to wear off at that point. I remember telling him that he should leave me alone if he wasn't going to give me the answers that might help me protect myself. We had arguments—okay, *I* argued with *him*—but Nine wouldn't budge. All he would say was that it was his job to protect me.

He promised me that my keeping him a secret would help with that. He reminded me again that, if I told anyone about him, he might not be able to come back. And I was mad, so, so mad at him, but he was my lifeline. I didn't really want him to go. So I kept my mouth shut.

That is, I kept my mouth shut until the Wilsons heard me talking to myself the nights that Nine visited me. They knew my story, knew that I had some issues, and they were just waiting for something like this to happen. They threatened me with therapy if I didn't explain myself.

So I did. They sent me to therapy anyway. When the first doctor mentioned the dreaded "s" word—*schizophrenia*—the Wilsons sent me away so fast, I never even got to pack my room up.

Dicks.

It worked out for me, though. For a little while, at least. Because up next? The Everetts.

They were experienced foster parents. They'd already adopted a girl they had fostered—Madelaine—and Mrs. Everett was an ER nurse. The Everetts thought they might be the home I'd been looking for my entire life. My history didn't frighten them. They swore they would get me any help I needed. I believed them.

And that's why I purposely didn't tell them about Nine when he eventually found me in Acorn Falls.

I was a contrary teenager with abandonment issues. I know that's no excuse, and I probably should have confided in them the first time I heard Nine whisper my name from the shadows. But he'd been there for so long, my loyalty was to the Shadow Man before anyone else.

He warned me again that my silence was imperative. As I grew older, I was only becoming more and more vulnerable. For some reason, the fae were still hunting me; in answer to my incessant questions, he said I'd know why in time, just not yet.

Still, it was important for me to remember the power of the touch. If any of them got their hands on me, they'd charm me and possess me and that would be the end of my life as I know it.

Turns out, Nine wasn't wrong.

Not even a little.

I DON'T SPEND MUCH TIME WITH THE OTHER patients. At first, it was because the doctors thought I would hurt them. Now? They're more concerned that I'll hurt myself.

I do get to spend breakfast with the others in my age group, and I have to participate in most of the group therapies: community group, which I hate, and recreational therapy, which is usually the best part of the day.

Today we're watching an old movie. It's in black & white and it has something to do with someone's missing bird. There's this hardass detective and some two-faced lady that even I can tell is bad news. I didn't think I would like it, even though Amy insists it's a classic, but it's pretty good.

It was actually getting kind of interesting when Amy angles the remote at the television, pausing the movie.

"Okay, guys. It's just about four o'clock. If you're expecting any visitors today, they're waiting for you in the meeting room. If you're not, then that's alright. You can stay with me and we'll watch the rest of the movie."

Ugh. My stomach drops. Visiting hour.

My least favorite hour of the whole day.

We have visiting hour daily, from four to five regular. It never changes. And since the facility's staff doesn't trust us to let any friends and family we might still have left into our ward, they designate an open room on the first floor for visiting hour. There are plenty of small tables and chairs set up down there so there's at least some semblance of privacy.

Not that it means anything to me.

Louis waits in the doorway. Nearly everyone in the group gets up and forms a line in front of him. Whether they know for sure that they're getting a visitor or they're just hoping, the others file out of the day room.

I don't. No point. I know there's no one out there for me.

Not anymore.

When I first got tossed into Black Pine, the Everetts would come to visit me from time to time. They moved away from Acorn Falls after the accident and now live in a city that's about six hours away by car. They couldn't visit me every day, but they tried to make it once a week to show me that they weren't giving up on me. With Madelaine gone, I was all they had left.

Of course, it didn't last long. Once a week turned into once a month until I noticed that Mr. and Mrs. Everett started to take the trip separately. About two years into my stay, I found out they had gotten divorced. The strain of Madelaine's death, plus my institutionalization, was just too much for them.

Before long, Mr. Everett stopped coming at all. The last time Mrs. Everett visited me, three Christmases ago, I pleaded with her to stop. It's bad enough I'm the reason they lost their child. It kills me that I'm to blame that they lost each other, too.

Mrs. Everett is a saint. I still get an occasional letter, not to mention gifts for my birthday and Christmas, and I'm good with that.

It's way more than I deserve.

Only two out of the twelve of us stay behind: me and Meg. That's not so new. Meg had visitors for a while, but a few months ago she stopped going down with the techs. I don't know why. I've never asked.

Amy waits until they're all gone to pick up the remote again. "You ladies want to finish the movie?"

I want to know who killed who. "Yeah."

Meg doesn't say anything. Since she doesn't shake her head no, Amy takes it as a yes. She turns the movie back on.

Out of the corner of my eye, I peek over at Meg. I don't know her story too well. Everybody inside has their quirks and their issues. Meg? She's mute. Everything I've learned about her is from the gossip that spreads from group to group, ward to ward. I heard that she was in a real bad accident with her brother and sister. She was the only survivor, but it messed her up. Physically, she's fine. That's why she's here with us instead of a regular hospital. She *could* speak, she just doesn't want to.

I get that.

It used to be me and Meg and Jason who stayed behind in the day room during visiting hour. He's still not around. I vaguely wonder for the second time what's happened to him.

But then the movie starts to get interesting again and I forget all about everything else.

———

Knock, knock.

I glance up from the book I'm reading. I know I heard that knock, but I wasn't expecting it. I had only just climbed into bed after hurrying through dinner. I thought reading a book might distract me enough that, even if I start hallucinating again, I can ignore it. Besides, I've read this one before. It's pretty good.

I set it down. My door's not locked—we don't get that luxury—but we do get to pretend that we have some choice when we're in our individual rooms.

"Yeah?"

"We're coming in, Thorne. Time for your nighttime meds."

Ugh. I recognize that rasp of a voice. Duncan.

He's early, too. Sure, it's June, and I know that days are longer in the summer, but a quick glance past the bars on my window shows that the sun's still out.

Weird. The nurses don't usually do the nighttime rounds until at least seven.

Oh, well. Could be that, since I turned in early, they decided to bring me my pills so they could get it out of the way. That's fine. I'm gonna take them, too.

I sure as hell don't want to dream tonight.

"Sure. Gimme a sec." After all these years, I know the drill. After I pull on my hoodie, tugging on my sleeves so that every bare inch of my arm is covered, I get up and move across the room. "Okay. Ready."

The door opens. Duncan peeks his head in, verifying that I'm not about to jump past him and make a break for it or something. Only once he decides that I'm not a risk will he step aside and let the nurse in while he watches over him or her.

At least, that's how he usually does it. Not tonight. For the first time ever, he goes against his normal routine. Instead of guarding the door like a bouncer, he strolls right into my room. He's not alone, either.

Long, blonde ponytail. Pale blue scrubs.

It's the tech from Sunday. Diana.

What's she doing here?

It doesn't make any sense. She's just a tech. Besides, it's Tuesday. Knowing my schedule and sticking to it is one of the things that keeps me sane inside of Black Pine. Just like how I know that Amy is off on Wednesdays and Saturdays so that Penelope is my main morning tech, I know which nurse to expect on Tuesday nights.

"Where's Nurse Stanley?"

"She's busy," answers Duncan. "We have the okay to give you your medications today."

My gut goes tight. It feels like someone twisted it up in a knot, grabbed both ends, and pulled. I *hate* this feeling. Even worse? I know exactly what caused it.

Duncan just lied to me.

"Are you sure about that?"

He nods. I'm watching him closely now, and I notice that something... something's really not right. His dark eyes are glazed over and he's wearing this crooked smile that doesn't seem normal. And maybe it's because I don't think I've ever seen Duncan smile before... I don't know. It's creepy, though, and I know he just lied to me again.

Diana approaches Duncan. She taps him on the shoulder and he crouches enough to allow her to whisper something to him. The big man nods. A second later, he disappears, leaving me alone with the blonde tech.

That's worse. I'm not sure why, but it seems worse. And there's nothing I can do about it.

I'm still not comfortable around her. She makes my fingers itch. I want to back up further, duck into the shadowy corner. I keep getting this feeling like she's about to reach out and grab me or something. She won't have my permission, but I don't think that would stop her.

I sidle along the wall at my back, watching her as she turns to smile over at me.

Just like my nighttime nurses always do, she's

carrying a tray with two cups. She picks one up, her smile never wavering. If she notices how I'm slowly moving away from her, she doesn't give any sign of it. She just holds the cup out toward me.

I take it. I have no choice. I snatch the cup out of her hand, careful not even to brush her skin with the edge of my glove. Then, once I've put space between us again, I look inside.

There's only one pill in the cup.

I blink. Nope. Still just one.

"Where the rest?" I ask.

I look down at the pill again. Yikes. I've never seen anything like it before. It's a horse pill, as big as a nickel, with a yellow center that looks wrong. The rest of the pill is white and speckled with green. It kind of reminds me of this mint Madelaine used to love. It definitely doesn't look like any sort of medication I've ever seen before.

I shake my head and offer it back. "Yeah, no. I'm not taking this."

"Oh? Is that so?" Diana's laugh is sickly sweet. "You'll take anything I tell you to."

I gasp—and it has nothing to do with what she just said to me.

Her eyes are hazel. I remember from Sunday. When I was on the floor of the day room, when she was trying to help me stand, I looked her in the eyes. They were hazel.

They're not anymore.

Now? They're a vivid, shining shade of gold.

There's no time for me to ease into one of my panic attacks. What happens next? This is full-blown hysteria.

I can't stop myself. As if I'm thrown back to the horrible afternoon when Madelaine died, I lash out. Totally out of control. I toss the cup, jamming the heel of my slipper against the pill. When it doesn't even break, I lunge forward, slapping the tray out of her hand.

Then, because I'm not even thinking a little bit, I back up, irrationally seeking the corner on the far side of my room. Once my back slams against one side, I wedge myself into the corner. In the back of my mind, I realize that all I did was trap myself even more—and Diana is watching me with those eerily familiar golden eyes.

I have to get out. I start banging on the wall.

I'm screaming, too. Don't know if I'm making sense or if it's just noise. The only thing I'm worrying about is how I'm going to get the hell away from Diana and her gold-colored eyes. The leather slaps against the wall, my right slipper flying off my foot as I flail. I need her to get back. I need her to stay away from me.

I crack the back of my head against the wall. The screams turn into screeches.

Duncan comes running in. He's certainly not smiling now. Head bowed, his body like a running back's, he leads with his shoulder, picking me up as easily as if I was a rag doll. Hell, I'm probably more of a rag doll than a living, breathing woman. I'm useless. I can't do anything except scream my lungs out, begging someone, anyone to save me from her.

It only gets worse when I realize that *Duncan is touching me*.

He tries to restrain me on my bed. I flop like a fish. He outweighs me by a good hundred pounds, but I'm fighting mad. He throws his weight around, pinning me down by my arms. I'm wild, but he has the leverage. I'm not going anywhere now.

I want to calm down. I really do. Except all I'm thinking about now is that he doesn't have my permission to touch me. He's making it all so much worse. Diana melts into the background as more and more people come pouring into my room.

Her eyes are still flashing gold.

I'm still screaming like a fucking banshee.

Over my shrieks, I can sort of make out Duncan's warnings. If I don't stop, he's going to get the straps. A white woman with wispy brown hair joins Duncan. That's the head nurse—Nurse Callahan—and she's trying in her no-nonsense way to organize the facility's staff. I'm still thrashing, trying to buck Duncan's weight off of me. When I feel another set of strong arms on my bare legs, I kick out with all of my strength.

I connect. I hear a sickening *crunch* when I hit someone. I don't know who. I'm in no state to give a shit.

The last thing I remember is the prick of the needle that one of the nurses plunges into my exposed calf. Even as I'm being sedated, the hysteria won't subside.

All I want to do is calm down enough to warn the staff that the monster that killed Madelaine is in the room with us all—but I can't.

As the medicine courses through me, I can't do anything at all.

CHAPTER 7

"**R**iley."

I hear my name. I know it's mine, even if there's a... a disconnect. Like, I know *I'm* Riley—but that's about *all* I know.

Where am I? It's dark and my head feels heavy. My body, too. It's almost like my arms and legs have been weighed down by something.

"*Wake up.*"

Am I sleeping? Makes sense. It would explain this woozy, weird feeling. Why fight it? I'll just lay here and sleep it off. Then, when I'm up again, I can forget the voice that's so clear and so close, it's like he's inside of my head.

"*Listen to me.*"

Is he still talking? I want to tell him no, that I don't want to listen to him, that I want him to go away, but I can't. My tongue is too thick in my mouth. I can't even screw open my jaw.

"Open your eyes."

No. That's impossible, too. My eyes feel like they're glued shut. I could probably pry my lids open if I wanted to.

I don't want to.

"Riley…"

Stop saying my name.

"I've missed you." The voice turns soft. Cajoling. It's a beautiful voice, lilting, like a lullaby. Despite not wanting to listen to him, I can't help it. Peace settles over me as most of my worries, anxieties, and discomfort simply melt away. *"It's been far too long."*

Who is he? Why does he sound like he knows me? It's been far too long… Though it feels like I should know who he is, I don't know his voice. It's so pretty, though. Anyone who sounds like that can't be all bad.

Right?

Wrong.

So, so wrong.

I blink my eyes open. The first thing I notice is that I'm not in my room. I'm lying in a bed—but it's not my bed, either. The blanket is softer, thicker than the one I have at Black Pine, and the sheets beneath my back feel like silk. The walls are painted a soft yellow—not industrial white—and the window to my right is missing its bars.

The second thing I notice?

I'm not alone.

As my eyes slide over to find the owner of that

lovely voice, fear comes rushing back, seizing control. I nearly choke.

Because there he is. The golden-eyed fae who killed my sister.

He's tall and unnaturally slender, just like I remember. From his side of the empty room, he looms over me, his shadow stretching out to cover the edge of this unfamiliar bed. His face… damn it, his every feature is breathtaking. Bronze skin, long golden hair, a body that would make an Olympic sprinter weep in shame.

He's beautiful, so angelically beautiful that I almost want to cry myself. In my mind, I always think of the golden fae as a monster. He doesn't look like one, though. He never has. It's his callous nature, his cold and capricious ways… it's how easily he killed Madelaine because I refused him… *that's* what makes him a monster.

Then there are his unnatural eyes—

His eyes are gold. Pure gold. They shine out from his face, his most mesmerizing feature of all. They're like two miniature suns burning bright as his lips curl in delight.

At first, I'm beyond terror. I'm so scared to see him standing there that I can't even scream. I'm paralyzed. Then I remember Diana had the same eyes as the ones set deep in his face.

The hysteria.

The sedation.

It's a dream.

No—a *nightmare*.

I shudder out a breath. Whatever he's doing here— no matter why I conjured him up during my drugged sleep—he can't hurt me and I *know* that.

Still, my voice shaky, I whisper, "It's you."

He holds out his hand. "Come to me."

Hell no. Not even in my dreams.

And it has to be a dream right now. I'm in an unfamiliar room with the monster from my memories and, while I know better than to get any closer to him, I'm not freaking out. Not really. I'm angry, sure, but also kinda calm. I've *got* to be dreaming. I mean, I have this hazy, vague feeling that I should be running, should be screaming, should be trying to escape—but I'm not. I'm just glaring over at this creature.

He's as terrifying as he is beautiful.

And then he shakes his head. His perfect lips tug into a frown.

He holds out his hand again.

"Zella. *Come*."

I don't know what it is that he said. Not the part where he orders me to come to him like I'm a dog or something—that part I've got. But that first word? It seems familiar, almost like I should know it, the way it sings in my ears and settles in my soul. I grasp at it, trying to capture it, but it disappears before I get the chance.

Besides, I'm a little bit preoccupied with my body's strange reaction to his command.

I actually *obey* the fae.

I don't have any control over my actions. Like a

puppet being manipulated by its strings, I rise from my lying position, my arms jerking wildly, my legs weak and wobbly. I swipe the blanket aside, then get to my feet. Once I'm standing, I try to dig in my heels. Doesn't work. Something is pulling me toward the golden fae—magic, charm, a compulsion—and it's too hard for me to fight against it.

I finally manage to break the spell when a precious few feet separate us. I shake my head, scrabbling backward so that he can't reach out and touch me. It won't stop him from striding closer, but I don't care about that right now.

I only care about the power he just showed me he has.

Though I can't tell you how he did it, I know his little display was on purpose. A calculated move to remind me that *he*'s in charge. That, despite every bone in my body refusing to willingly move toward him, he has the magic and the strength to command me to go to him—and I *did*.

That scares me more than knowing I'm in the same room as him.

I swallow back my frightened gasp. "What did you just do to me?"

"You made me do it." He can't deny it—we both know he was responsible for dragging me from my bed —but I'm not surprised to hear him blame me. Of course it's my fault. The fae are never wrong. "I need you to understand this. There's too much at stake here. I don't want to have to compel you to listen to me, but

I will if you force my hand. Time is short and I've come for you as I promised."

He did. Six years ago, when he sacrificed Madelaine because I told him to leave us the hell alone, he promised that he would return. That he would come back for me.

In the safety of my dreams, I let myself think back. He might have control here—but he can't hurt me while I sleep. It's not how it works. It's not how any of this works. He can talk to me, he can show off his magic tricks, he can remind me of promises—of *threats* —that I've long since buried… and that's all.

The golden fae is the reason I allowed myself to accept that the fae were nothing more than an elaborate hallucination because I was mentally unwell. If I made them up, then I didn't have to worry about them chasing after me for the rest of my life. I wouldn't have to spend years looking over my shoulders.

I'd be able to forget his sworn promise that he'd come for me again one day.

And now he's here and, instead of panicking or closing my eyes to shut him out, I'm watching him closely, absolutely sure that he is as real as anyone else I've ever known.

I shake my head. "This can't be happening. You're not supposed to be *real*."

"And you're not supposed to resist me."

That's all thanks to Nine. If he hadn't warned me what the fae were capable of back when I was a kid, I would've been lost the first time I met this monster. I saved myself then—it was Madelaine who paid the price for the fae's interest in me.

And now he's back.

"Why? Why me? What do you *want* from me?"

"I've waited long enough. It's time that you become my *ffrindau*."

His *what*? It's another unfamiliar word in a strange, harsh accent that is at odds with his lyrical voice. I don't think it's English, but if it is? There's only one word that sounds like that that I know.

"Friends? You want me to be your *friend*? You've got to be fucking kidding me!"

His golden eyes flash. His lips curve as he peers down at me. The fae is wearing a… a hungry look that has me stepping away from him again.

That doesn't stop him. Honestly, I'm not sure if there's anything I could do to him that would.

He glides toward me. Everything about him is graceful, peaceful, lovely—but I know better. I'm staring up at a man-eater who doesn't know whether he wants to toy with me first, or go straight for the kill.

"Stay away from me." I throw my hands up in warning. "Back off— *whoa*."

As if I needed another clue that this has to be a dream, I get one when I see my hands.

My *bare* hands.

I'm not wearing my gloves. I *always* wear my gloves.

It's bright where we are. The light shines on my mottled skin. I marvel at the blotches, the scars, the fine lines, and the raw pink patches that mingle with the once-damaged flesh. Looking at my reconstructed hands is even worse than coming face to face with the golden fae.

At least, when I wake up in the morning, he'll be gone. I'll have these hands forever.

I remember a time when my hands were my own, not these monstrosities. Back before me and Madelaine decided we should skip school that Monday morning and hang out in the basement of an abandoned house down the street from the Everetts. Back before the golden fae appeared out of thin air and convinced Madelaine to dance with him, no matter how much I begged her not to. Back before the fire and the pain and the realization that Nine hadn't lied, that the fae and all of Faerie was real.

The fae don't live by the same rules that we do. They can hurt you—and they *will*.

I made a mistake. Staring at my ruined palm, letting the memories distract me from what the hell is going on right now, I made a huge mistake. I sense movement, a rustle of the wind, and when my head jerks up, he's right there.

He holds up his hand. His perfect, bronze-colored hand. Fingers pointed up, palm facing out.

"Dance with me, Riley."

I almost hurl.

Dance with me, Riley.

He knew my name then, too. He commanded me to dance, then he commanded me to leave with him, and I refused. Just like now, my refusal surprised him that day in the basement. I tried to warn Madelaine, I tried to tell her that he was beautiful, but he was fae, and that made him more dangerous than anything she'd ever known before.

Sometimes, on my worse days, I remember the look of betrayal in her big brown eyes the instant before he took her hand, then snapped her neck.

"Never."

"Zella. *Dance*."

There's that word again. I hear it and I'm helpless to do anything except obey.

Under the sway of his power, I lift my hand and press my palm against his. I don't know what's worse: the spark, the sizzle when our bare skin touches, or how his long, lean perfect fingers make mine look like they belong on Frankenstein. My stomach twists. My mouth clamps shut, choking on a silent scream. I try to yank my hand back and I can't. I just *can't*.

His other hand is a brand on my hip. I feel the heat through my Black Pine tee. When he pulls me closer, lining my front along his lean, muscular body, it's like I'm burning up inside. He's full of fire and temptation, burning bright as the sun, and his golden eyes flash as he tilts his head, gobbling me up with his gaze.

"Zella," he murmurs again. "Stay with me."

I give in. I can't fight it. Knowing it's a dream, praying that this doesn't mean a thing, I recognize that some part of me doesn't want to pull away from him. For years, I used to hate Madelaine for giving up so easily, falling prey to this monster's charm before he snapped, but I can't help myself. Everything from his soft voice to his mesmerizing eyes is hypnotic. If he killed me right now, I don't think I would do a single thing to stop it.

I don't like the idea of dying. I want to live. In two weeks... two weeks and a couple of days... I'll be released from the asylum. Not free, though. His hand against mine, his body against mine, his soft voice echoing around me as he starts to sing... I figure out something that will be devastating when this dream is over.

Now that the golden fae has found me again? I'll *never* be free.

Music starts to play. A soft hum, it tickles my ears, makes me forget that I'm playing with fire. Literally. I've seen the golden fae create enchanted fire with the snap of his fingers. It's how I burned my hands, after all. After throwing Madelaine's broken body on the floor, he surrounded her in a circle of fire, daring me to save my sister.

I couldn't save Madelaine then. Something tells me that there's no saving me now, either.

So I dance.

It's easy to lose myself in the sensation. With his help, I move so lightly that it's as if I'm drifting up off of the floor. He laughs softly in time to the music, a mix of a chuckle and a sigh.

I keep my eyes closed so that I don't have to look at his.

I don't know how long we're dancing for when he

speaks again. I hear him clearly, his mouth right next to my cheek as he whispers, "You know what I am."

I've always known. "Yes."

"But you don't know *who* I am."

I know enough. He's the golden fae. A monster. The creature who killed Madelaine.

The creature who's trying to seduce me right now.

I'm not innocent. I'm not all that naive, either. I wasn't always in a good foster home; I spent the long months in between in the system, bouncing from group homes to institutions. I lost my virginity at thirteen with an older boy before I went to live with the Everetts, before my haphephobia got so bad. When I could give permission, I actually *liked* being touched. It's just... when you start to see monsters everywhere, it's hard to know who to trust.

I know better than to trust him. A dance is just a dance, even if the way he's moving right now reminds me of so much more.

But not with him. Never with him.

He presses closer.

"Do you want to know who I am?" he whispers.

Hell no.

I shake my head again, so frantically that his lips kiss my ear. It burns and I try to pull away.

He holds me tighter.

"So be it," he concedes. "But know this: I will always come for you."

I don't know if he means that as a promise or a

threat. Some of the fog lifts. The words... I've heard them before. From him? I'm... I'm not sure.

The music grows louder, as if trying to drown out my thoughts. My heart is beating in time to it. I try to focus. The magic is fading, my senses returning. What the fuck am I doing? I push with my free hand, yanking with the other. His grip is so strong, I begin to suspect that he'll never let me go.

We're spinning now. When I finally find the strength to open my eyes, everything is a blur of gold and white. I don't know how far I fell under his spell. Pretty damn far and I'm still trying to crawl out from under it as we go faster and faster. He slips his fingers between mine. Another touch.

"Don't fight it—don't fight *me*. You're safe now. I'll never hurt you."

A shiver courses through me. Or maybe it's him. I'm trembling as he saps all of my strength. Not only do I stop fighting, I actually lean into his embrace. I'm not sure I can support myself without holding onto him.

I wait for the twist in my belly that tells me that he's lying to me. The fae can't lie, but how can I believe him after he killed Madelaine?

I can't—but my stomach stays settled.

He means every damn thing he says to me.

———

I don't know how long I'm sleeping for but, when I finally come out of my sedation, I wake up to the sound of music in my head. It takes me a second before my dream rushes to the front of my mind.

When it does, I pop up in my bed like a panicked jack-in-the-box. I lift my hands high, putting them in front of my face, flipping them back and forth until I'm sure that they're both covered all of the way with my leather gloves.

Because it *was* a dream. Just a dream brought on by the sedatives.

There was no golden fae. No dance. It was a terrible, strange nightmare that I forced my broken brain to live through after the way I hallucinated that the blonde tech had eyes just like the golden fae. I imagined her hazel eyes were gold, and paid for it by being sedated by the nursing staff.

At least I didn't wake up strapped down. That's a plus. And there's weak light streaming in past the six bars on my window. It's morning.

But *which* morning?

I get my answer shortly. It's Amy who comes in and does my vitals. Just seeing her is a big clue that I lost more time than I thought. If she's here, then it's Thursday at the earliest. I lost all of Wednesday.

She confirms it as she rattles on, going a mile a minute as if she's trying to make up for the time I was out. Not once does she mention my sedation, though she swiftly checks the bruising where they jabbed me with the needle before she covers the purple lump with a fresh bandage.

I wait until she takes a breath before I ask her the only thing I care about.

"Where's the other tech? Where's Diana?"

Especially on the heels of my strange dream, I know I never want to go near her again. The dream put things into perspective for me; with a clear head, it's a relief to realize I had been seeing things. The flash of gold I saw in her eyes? It must have been a trick of the setting sun since it *was* early when Diana and Duncan came to bring me my medicine.

Still, just the thought of coming face to face with her again—just the chance that maybe I'll see that flash again—has my breath picking up. It's a little more labored than it was before.

Amy looks touched, almost like she mistook my worry for concern or something. I wonder if she got my motives wrong.

Yeah. She totally did.

"Oh, Riley." She goes to pat my hand, remembers in an instant which patient I am, then pats the edge of my bed instead. "It's so sweet of you to worry about Diana."

Sweet? Nope. More like covering my own ass. I can't have another attack like that. I'm so close to getting out of the asylum. I'm not about to let anything jeopardize that. I could just see it now. The nursing staff and the techs tell the doctors that I'm a threat and, look at that, my release gets put on hold. Instead of going to the transition house, I get referred to an adult facility.

I can't let that happen.

"Where is she?" I ask again.

Amy frowns, like she has bad news and doesn't want to share it. My pulse picks up, settling only after she tells me, "Well, the truth is that she was transferred out of your age group yesterday. Now, don't blame yourself, okay? Things happen. It's not your fault."

From the tiniest twinge at the bottom of my stomach, I know Amy is lying. It's a kindness, though. She's actually trying to make me feel better.

Because Diana getting tossed off our floor?

We both know that it *is* my fault.

CHAPTER 8

No rain today.

I peeked out of my window before I shimmied off my hoodie, tossed it onto my dresser, and followed Amy into the hall. I know it's not raining, and the morning message says some motivational bullshit about sunshine in our lives so I know it's another gorgeous sunny day that I'm missing out on.

The morning passes me by in a haze. I'm jumpy, the last of the sedatives working their way out of my system. It makes me feel off, and it's only worse when I notice a couple of the other patients watching me closely.

It makes me antsy. *I'*m supposed to be the people-watcher.

Their stares have me hunching my shoulders, ducking as I walk, anxiously tugging on my gloves as I pretend not to see them gaping in open interest at me.

107

My daily check-in is a lecture. I'm not looking forward to my meeting with Lorraine the next time I see her. No doubt that Black Pine informed her about my meltdown as soon as they sedated me. I'm starting to get worried that what happened the other night's gonna affect my chances of getting released on time. I spend most of lunch toying with my meal, trying to come up with a good excuse for how I reacted when Diana tried to bring me my meds.

One thing for sure? I'm not about to admit that, for a second there, I thought she was the golden fae in disguise. Especially since I can still feel the heat of his hand against mine from the dance we shared while I was under.

I don't know what kind of group therapy I was expecting that afternoon. It's not raining, but a cheery therapist named Tonya claps her hand and insists we try some more creative therapy. She's too new to realize that it's a real bad idea to treat our age group like we're some kind of democracy. When she offers to let us vote, most of the therapy session is wasted when half the group wants music therapy and the rest decide on art.

Now, I'm not a big fan of art therapy. I've always thought it was a waste of time, especially for our group. But if it's art therapy or music? I'm going art. Just the idea of a music therapy session is a trigger for me after last night.

Nope. If I never hear another note again, I'm good.

The vote is a joke. We're split down the middle, six

to six. I blame Whitney for that. She kept quiet at first, only making her vote when she figured out it would create a tie. I'm not surprised. That's Whitney for you. She gets a kick out of watching our group argue like children, a real shit-starter.

I'm so not in the mood.

"I don't care about the rest of the group," I announce to the room, "but I won't do music therapy. Get a tech. Take one of my points. I don't care. I won't do it."

Tonya is new to Black Pine, but she's an experienced therapist. I might not test that way, but my refusal today is a clear example of ODD. Oppositional Defiant Disorder. No matter what she says, she can't make me.

Her voice immediately adjusts. Instead of happy and go-lucky, she's suddenly calm. As if her soothing tone will get me to change my mind.

"Riley, we're going to decide as a group. Whatever the group decides, that's what we're going to do. I hope you understand."

I huff. That's not going to work. Sorry.

"Umm… excuse me?" Carolina raises her hand. "I'd like to change my vote. Can I do that? I… I don't mind art therapy."

Lie.

That's a lie.

And I don't even need the twinge that hits my stomach to know that. Everyone in our group was there the last time we had art therapy. Carolina's sobbing fit was the talk of the ward the whole rest of that night. Why would she switch her vote?

I glance over at her. Though she was talking to Tonya, her dark eyes are locked on me. Carolina is watching me.

And I know exactly why she switched her vote.

"Thank you, Carolina. Now it's seven-six—and, no, Whitney, that's it for changed votes. Art therapy it is. Ready? Let's go."

Along with her idea of democracy, Tonya gives instructions that are supposed to be liberating—but they're just kinda vague. She tells us to grab some paper, some crayons, then draw whatever our hearts tell us to.

Jeez.

Another rookie mistake with a group like ours.

I can already imagine what some of the other patients are gonna draw. She didn't even reiterate our normal rules about keeping it clean and violence-free.

I didn't mean to be such a pain before, and I know I'm already walking on thin ice. I'm not about to push any of the staff by drawing something inappropriate. She wants me to let my creativity flow? Okay. I can try.

Today, I grab a sheet of black construction paper. I grab a couple of crayons, then choose the yellow crayon first. Putting the tip to the dark paper, I start to doodle aimlessly. No real direction or anything. In fact, I'm barely even paying attention as the half-hearted, absent strokes start to develop into something very familiar.

Yellow skin, yellow hair, yellow eyes. Without even

meaning to, I've drawn a caricature of the golden fae from my dream.

When I catch on to what I've done, I tear the paper into six equal strips, then start ripping each strip into five pieces. Within seconds, there's nothing left but thirty black squares, some with an indistinguishable yellow squiggle running through it.

If only I could erase the monster from my mind as easily as that.

At the end of the session, Tonya is disappointed that I have nothing to share. Turns out she doesn't think that making confetti is constructive or creative so, after Carolina switched just to help me out, I still lose credit for the hour's session. Amy makes a note on my chart. I'm sure Lorraine or my case manager will ask me about that, too.

Great.

Fucking great.

———

THAT NIGHT, DINNER IS BROUGHT TO MY room. I don't even get the chance to eat with the rest of the group.

I expected it. They think they're punishing me for my outburst on Tuesday night, but I prefer it—even if it means Nurse Stanley is the one who keeps me company while I eat.

She leaves when I'm finished, taking my tray with her. She isn't gone long, though. About an hour later, she comes back to do my nighttime vitals, bringing my meds with her. No Duncan tonight, though. Frankie follows her in the room, paying me close attention as if he's waiting for me to flip out any second now.

Whatever. It's been a long day and I'm exhausted. When Nurse Stanley places my cups on the dresser, I peek inside just long enough to make sure they're my regular meds before tossing them back.

Of course, when I *want* them to, the damn things don't work.

I lose track of how long I lay awake in my bed, unable to fall asleep. I don't have a clock in my room. I've never needed one. With the techs acting as my alarm clock on the rare occasion that I don't wake up on my own, it seemed like a waste.

Apart from my dresser with my hoodie folded on top, my bed, and my nightstand, my room is empty. I didn't bring a book with me tonight and, besides, it's 'lights out'. The moon is full, hanging high in the sky. It's bright, but it's not bright enough to allow me to read.

Instead, I lay flat on my back, blanket pulled up to my chin, and watch the moon through my barred windows. Dark clouds roll across the sky like liquid ink. Hours pass. I'm still not tired.

I'm beginning to wonder if we'll be in for another storm tomorrow when I hear the faintest rustle and freeze.

No, I tell myself. It *can't* be.

"*Riley.*"

I immediately close my eyes. A second later, I lift my hands out from under my blanket and clamp them over my ears.

No, no, no.

Not again.

It should have worked. The leather gloves, plus how tightly I'm pressing my palms to my ears… it should have worked. No way I should be able to hear anything other than the frantic drumming of my frightened heart.

But then I hear, almost as if he's annoyed—

"Don't be ridiculous. I know you're still awake."

Of course I am. Who knows how long he was watching me before he made a move? That's the thing about Nine. He was always so quiet. He could've been here for as long as the moon's been out, I don't know. I remember that about him. He never let me know he was there until *he* was ready to announce his presence.

Like the way he whispered my name.

If he'd been watching me, he would've seen me with my eyes open, staring out of my window. He would've seen my reaction, watched me as I covered my ears and shut my eyes.

It's a good thing that only a few seconds have passed. When I open my eyes again, they're still adjusted to the dark and the gloom. I pull myself up into a sitting position, resting on my forearms, searching for the owner of the voice I know all too well.

The other day, I refused to acknowledge him. I swallowed my pills and went to sleep and pretended that

Nine hadn't come to see me for the first time in six years. But that was the other day. After what happened the last time I slept—well, was sedated—I think part of me was waiting for Nine to return.

The golden fae found me. Maybe it was only a matter of time before I conjured up my Shadow Man again.

I know every inch of this room. If he's here, I know exactly where to find Nine. My eyes are drawn to the deepest, darkest shadows where two of the walls meet in a corner.

And there he is.

I've never forgotten what Nine looked like. I know all about glamour, of course, the fae's ability to appear however they want to, but Nine has always appeared the same. He was tall, slender, an ageless beauty. His skin was pale, almost ghostly so, a stark contrast to his midnight hair. He had a sculpted face, all harsh angles with an unforgiving mouth.

Nine never smiled.

He's not smiling now, either. His silver eyes flash and gleam, a pair of headlights beaming through the darkness of my room. He's staring at me. He doesn't seem to blink at all. I get the crazy idea that he's too busy watching me to close his eyes for even a second.

That's okay. I'm not blinking, either.

This… this isn't how I remember Nine.

It's him. No doubt about that. Still tall, slender, his body cloaked in a long, black coat that swishes in the shadows as he dares to take a few steps closer. A sliver of moonlight falls on his face.

I gasp.

He's stunning. Like, I'm sitting in my bed, staring at him, *stunned* stunning. Holy shit. I don't know if I've ever seen anyone who looks as good as he does. And, okay, I always harbored a crush on him. Why wouldn't I? He was the only guy I knew who actually seemed to care about me when I was younger, but his perfection was a little off-putting. Plus there was the whole age difference and power dynamic. I was a kid. Nine was a Shadow Man.

Now he's one hell of a man.

Whoa.

His hair is different, too. The last time I saw him, he'd grown it out to his chin. Now it falls a few inches past his shoulders. It looks so soft. I just want to run my fingers through its length.

But that would be touching. And Nine was very clear on his no touching rule.

Wait—*no*. I can't let myself fall into this obvious trap. I managed to make it through six years without him. I worked hard to put him behind me, to pretend that the Faerie realm with its magic and its threats were stories I made up during a lonely, unstable childhood.

I've been pretending so long, I don't even know what's real anymore.

My panic attacks? They're real.

The anxiety and terror when it comes to someone grabbing me without my permission? That's real, too.

The Shadow Man might be just as real as my diagnoses—he certainly looks real to me right now—but I can't act like I believe that. That's a one-way ticket straight to Black Pine's adult facility.

Nope.

It can't be Nine.

He disappeared when Madelaine died and all of Acorn Falls heard me blame the fae.

I don't know where he went. Don't know why he's back, or why he's trying to talk to me again right after I dreamed of the golden fae.

I sure as hell don't like it, though.

Squinting in the gloom, I meet his unblinking gaze. Besides being stunned by his radiant beauty, I'm so scared by what his sudden appearance could mean. I'm angry, too. I'm not panicking yet, but that's probably because I'm actually kinda shocked that he's visiting me for the first time in years, plus I have this urge to throw myself into his arms.

No. No touching.

I slide my gloved hands under my ass. If I'm sitting on them, he can't touch me—and I can't reach for him.

Then, swallowing back the ball of emotions that are lodged in my throat, I snap, "What are you staring at?"

Because he *is* staring. And, okay, there are probably a hundred other things I could have said to acknowledge him—something like, "Who the hell are you, stranger in my bedroom," since I'm not about to admit I remember him—but his stare is bothering me.

"It's been a long time," he says in answer. Long time? No shit. "You look different."

I do? Well, so does he.

"What are you doing here?" I demand.

"Don't tell me you've forgotten about me."

Nine's voice is soft, lyrical, alluring. Just like the golden fae. But it's harsh too, like it used to be. It always made me think he was mad at me. Whenever it softened, I felt like I won a prize.

The harsh edge grates against the last of my nerves. "How can I forget you?" I demand. "There's no *you* to forget. Anyway, I made you up when I was a kid. You shouldn't be here!"

I can't believe what I'm seeing. For years, I believed in him—trusted him, *loved* him—and then he was gone. For years, I've been lectured, coached, medicated, and convinced that he never existed. And, yet, here he is. My imaginary friend, almost exactly as he was back then, standing a few feet away from me.

I wonder, if I yell loud enough, will the sound carry through the wall? Probably not. I could bang on the door, hope that one of the overnight nurses is passing by. Would they help me? Or only sedate me again?

I don't scream. Just in case. I *don't* scream.

But I whisper. "No. *No.* You… know what? You're not real. You're not. You're a hallucination, that's all. You shouldn't be here. I took my pills."

"I assure you, I'm as real as you are." He hesitates

before extending his arm. His skin is so pale, it seems to glow in the moonlight. "Touch me and prove it to yourself."

A hysterical laugh bubbles up and out of my throat. "Ha! If you really were Nine, you'd tell me not to touch you at all."

He smiles. The simple quirk of his lush lips has my stomach tied up in knots. Nine's grin is even worse than Dr. Gillespie's—but for totally different reasons.

"Ah," he says softly, "so you *do* remember."

Suddenly, I'm twelve again, smiling adoringly up at Nine, preening because his voice has gentled. No, no. *No.* I'm older now and, if not wiser, then definitely wary. I've only got two weeks until I'm twenty-one and I can put this all behind me.

I push away, scoot back, slamming my head, my neck, my back against the wall behind me. I slip my hands out from under my ass, clutching the hem of my blanket, yanking it so that it covers me to my belly button. I'm wearing my Black Pine tee to sleep like I always do and the bared skin on my arms has me wishing I had the will to get up and get my hoodie.

I can't, though. I'm still stunned, frozen in my bed.

Nine is waiting for me to say something.

So I do.

"What are you doing here?"

The smile fades. His expression goes stony, his silver eyes dimming noticeably. "You were supposed to be safe. No one should have been able to track you here, but... it's time, Shadow. They found you. She knows where you are."

They.

The fae.

I've spent almost twenty years waiting for them to find me. Last night, the golden fae male followed me into my dream.

At least, I *thought* it was a dream.

Wasn't it?

Shadow... god, I haven't heard that name in so long. I missed it. I didn't even realize how much I did until Nine threw it out there like that, another way to remind me that—whether or not I've made him up— we have a history together. Shadow. Because he only came at night, because he stayed to the shadows himself, it made me feel so precious that he cared enough to give me a name that reminded me of him.

Even though I've been Riley Thorne since my first foster family, I used to love being Nine's Shadow.

Right now, though? I would gladly never hear that name again if it meant that he hadn't just said that the fae have found me. My whole life, the fae have always been my very own personal bogeymen. For reasons I've never been told—because Nine always insisted I was too young to learn them—the fae have been hunting me for years. At least, that's what I let myself believe.

Because, you know, this isn't real.

I cling to that certainty. What else can I do?

Nine has an answer for that. "Come on. Get up. We have to go. You have to leave with me."

Leave? Doesn't he see the bars on my window? "What? No. I can't."

"But you can." His silver eyes flash hypnotically. "I'll show you. Now give me your hand."

I almost do, too. There's something about the way he said that, so simple, so insistent… I have my right glove halfway off before I realize what I am about to do.

I shake my head, clearing it. Angrily, I yank my glove back on. "Don't do that!"

"Do what?" he asks.

"You know what! You're trying to trick me."

"I'm trying to *save* you. It's all I've ever done. It's all I can do."

He's not real, he's not real…

The chanting inside my head doesn't help. Nine's still standing there.

"Let me prove it. Don't you want to know why I've come back now? I've just learned that this place isn't safe for you anymore."

Um. Does he really not see the bars on the window? My door's locked. No one can get to me—

Before I can point that out, he says, "They've already made themselves known to you, haven't they? I'm not the first from Faerie that's come to see you. Am I right?"

He's not real, he's not r—

"How did you know that?"

He blinks. I think it might've been the first time since he stepped out of the shadows that he shutters his eyes before opening them wide again. The silver shines, illuminating the dark expression on his beautiful face.

"I didn't know," he says roughly. "But I feared it. Rys got to you first."

"Reese?" The single syllable sends a shiver down my spine. "Who's Reese?"

Nine shakes his head, long hair rippling down the back of his coat. "There's no time. When it comes to you, I can't even trust my kind not to interfere. A Seelie? Impossible. You've got to come with me. We'll talk later."

Yeah. No. "I'm locked in an asylum, having an argument with one of my hallucinations. I think I can decide if there's enough time or not."

Nine scowls. It doesn't do a damn thing to make him look any less gorgeous. "You know very well that I'm not a hallucination."

I ignore that. He's right, of course. My meds are supposed to keep them away, yet here he is, even after I took my complete dose. I reach over and pinch my arm. It *hurts*. There goes the hope that I fell asleep without realizing it and this is all another crazy dream.

"Either tell me what you're talking about or go. Who the hell is Rys and why should I care that he's after me?"

"Not after you. He already knows where you are. He can take you away whenever he wants to. That's why you have to come with me now. You can't let him get his hands on you. He'll do anything for a touch."

Anything? Like, I don't know, use magic to step into

my dream, make my gloves disappear, and compel me to dance with him while pressing his palm against mine?

Uh-oh.

I think back to last night, the terrible dream with the golden fae. How he asked me if I knew what he was, then who he was. I didn't.

I guess I do now.

"Rys... is that the name of the monster who killed my sister?"

Nine frowns. "He's not a monster. Rys is a fae—"

Obviously. I already figured out that part. "Yeah? Tell me something I don't know."

"—like me."

My jaw drops.

Okay, then.

I definitely didn't know *that*.

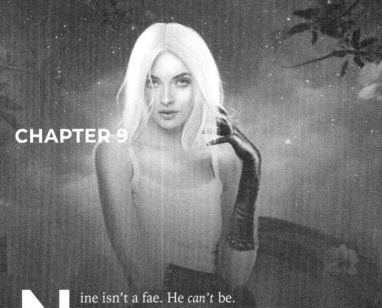

Nine isn't a fae. He *can't* be.

If anything, he's my Shadow Man: part bogeyman, part guardian angel. The one who spent my whole childhood warning me about the fae. Not once, in all those years, did he ever admit he was part of the race he was protecting me from.

"What? No… *no*. That's not right."

"Sorry to disappoint you. I thought you knew. I never hid what I was—"

"I would've remembered if you told me you were one of them!"

Nine doesn't say anything. He just bows his head, shielding his strange silver eyes, letting his long, wavy black hair fall forward like a shield.

He's gorgeous, no denying that. Just like the golden fae, Nine is absolute perfection. But they look nothing alike. They're total opposites, even if they do have total disdain for humans in common.

That's something I *do* remember. As my hands burned, my throat raw from screaming, I remember the puzzled look on the golden fae's face—on Rys's face—as he said, "She was just a human."

As if that made her life worth less than his. As if that made *my* life worth less because I'm a human.

My whole childhood, Nine didn't hide the fact that he was purposely looking past me being a human in order to help me. I thought it was because he was something totally different than what he was warning me about. A Shadow Man, a creature tied to Faerie who had his own motives, his own magic.

I never thought he was part of the ruling race. Or that he was teaching me to protect myself from his kind.

"How can you be a fae, too? You don't look anything like the other one."

"There's no time for this—"

I need to understand. "Make time or get the hell out of my room. You're the one who told me to stay away from the fae."

"Except for me. Listen, I can explain in detail when I've gotten you somewhere safe."

Bullshit. "I'm safe right here."

"Riley—"

I can't do this right now. I *can't*. "Know what? Forget it. I don't want to hear anything else from you. You abandoned me six years ago and I did just fine without you. I don't know why you decided to come back now, but you wasted both of our time. Just go."

"Riley—"

"I'll scream," I threaten.

"You have to forget this nonsense and come with me. You don't have any idea how much trouble you're in right now."

"Yeah? And why's that? Because you won't tell me. You've never told me anything except to keep my hands to myself and guess what, Nine?" I show him my gloves. "That didn't work out so great, did it?"

"Very well." Nine glances over his shoulder, peering into the inky blackness of the shadow as if he's searching for something. He nods. "You're not wrong. Dawn isn't for a few hours yet in the human world. There's some time. Ask your questions. I vow to answer them if I can if that's the proof you need to trust me on this."

Trust Nine when I just discovered the truth about him? Yeah, he's got a snowball's chance in hell of that happening.

But I also recognize that I've backed him into a corner. For some reason, he's desperate to get me to agree to leave with him. He thinks answering my questions will make me trust him again?

Sure. Let's go with that.

Hey. The fae can't lie, but humans sure can.

"How are you both fae?"

"Don't you remember how I told you there were two kinds of fae?"

Now that he mentions it, I kinda do. "The Cursed and the Blessed."

He nods. "That's right. The Cursed Ones are the Unseelie, the Blessed Ones the Seelie. Two different races make up the same people, all of us lorded over by the Fae Queen."

"So you're saying there's good and bad types. Blessed and cursed." My heart skips a beat. "Which one are you?"

"It's not as simple as that. Good and bad... no. I've told you this before, Riley. Those are human concepts. In Faerie, it comes down to Light and Dark. One rules during the time of the sun, the other when the moon is out. It's when we are at our strongest, that's all it means."

I don't have to ask which one he is again.

Dark Fae. Nine's skin is ghostly white, his eyes that freakish silver, but his hair is midnight black and he wears the shadows like a second skin. Plus, he always made sure I knew that he could only come to the human world at night.

And now I finally know what the beautiful monster is.

A Light Fae. Golden eyes, golden hair, golden skin. He lit the house on fire during the afternoon—in the sunlight.

Rys must be part of the Seelie class then, the Blessed Ones.

Okay, Nine totally just made his point. No way would anyone ever consider Madelaine's killer a good guy. And Nine, as dark as he might be, has only ever been kind to me.

I'm just about to ask him *why* when he continues and I don't get the chance.

"Just because he's a Light Fae, a Seelie, don't make the mistake in thinking he's not dangerous. He's still a fae, and one who will stop at nothing to get what he desires."

Has Nine forgotten about everything Rys has cost me so far? Madelaine, my poor hands, and the last six years in the asylum?

I'll never forget for a second how dangerous he is.

I show Nine my gloves again. "Yeah. I know."

"Do you really? He was just playing then. You were a child, nothing more. Last night, he hunted you down, stole another touch. It only made him stronger. It'll get worse when you hit your twenty-first birthday."

Because they're letting me out of Black Pine, I guess, and Rys will have an easier time looking for me. But how the hell does *Nine* know that?

Pretending like I'm not suddenly spooked by the idea of Rys forever searching for me, I shrug. "I still have more than two weeks until then to worry about my birthday."

A strange expression flashes across his face, there and gone again. For a second, it looks like he's about to argue with me before he changes his mind.

Shaking his head, long hair spilling down the back of his strange coat, Nine says, "Rys is even more dangerous now. A fae who has set his eyes on a lover is often ruthless and the laws say—"

A too-loud chuckle bursts out of me. "A lover? Oh, come on."

"You must take this seriously, Riley. He's convinced himself that he wants you."

Dance with me.

Stay with me.

I'll always come for you.

He said those words to me when I was fifteen. He said them again last night, and so much more. The way he pressed his body against mine, the way his lips brushed my ears, how he moved like he was trying to claim me while I was too enchanted to pull away from him.

Suddenly, I'm not laughing any longer.

Because it wasn't a dream. It was a seduction, and I don't know how far I let him take it.

From the look on Nine's face, I'm thinking way, way too far.

"No. You've got that all wrong. He... he's sorry about Madelaine. That's all it is. He just wants to be my friend."

The air whistles as Nine draws in a short breath. His cheekbones are so sharp, they could slice through paper. Eyes flashing, he demands, "Rys said that to you?"

Didn't he? "Well, yeah."

"Friend. He said *friend*?"

"Something like that."

Nine looms over me, his expression darker than it

has been. "This is important. What did the Light Fae tell you?"

"I don't know. Hang on. It was—" Come on. What was that weird word he used again? It sounded so much like 'friend', but foreign. Too bad Allison is down the hall. She'd be able to help me figure it out. It was almost German... I shrug. "Friend-ow. Maybe."

Nine pales. Seriously. I mean, the guy's already super white. Now, though? He loses any color he has left.

"*Ffrindau?*"

That's it. "Yeah. Why? I get that it's bad—no way I want to be friends with a psycho fae killer, but at least he's not chasing after me like all you other monsters."

His scowl returns with a vengeance. I'm not sure if it's because I made a point to lump him in with the other fae—he's fae, I still can't believe that my Shadow Man is one of *them*—or because I'm not letting the golden fae bother me as much as I used to. In my dream, he promised me he'd never hurt me and, one thing I know for sure, it's that the fae can't lie.

Which is why I'm stunned at what Nine says next. Because, as much as I wish it wasn't the truth, I know it must be.

"*Ffrindau* doesn't mean friend. It's an ancient term from a dead Faerie language that still lives on today. If Rys thinks of you as his *ffrindau*, you're in even more trouble than if he was hoping to capture you on behalf of the Fae Queen."

My heart just about stops beating. "Really? Why? What does... what does that word mean?"

"It means mate. soulmate, to be precise."

"Soul *what?*"

Nine clenches his jaw so tightly, I can see a muscle tic. "Mate. He doesn't want to be your friend. He wants you to be his bonded mate for all eternity, whether you're meant to be his or not."

There's something in the way he says that. When I was a kid, I always understood that Nine knew tons more than the little bit he told me. He had all the power then—if he wanted to guard his secrets, there wasn't a damn thing I could do about it.

It's different now. I'm older, tougher, and I'm teetering on the edge of a massive breakdown. I spent six years convincing myself that the fae weren't real. Now, when I'm so close to being free, to putting my nightmares behind me—as if I really *could*—now I have to deal with this?

The fae can't lie. Nine's finally confessed that he's one of the Faerie folk, so he can't lie, either. He can twist the truth any which way he wants to. In the end, no matter what, it'll be the truth.

I'm at my breaking point. He knows more than he's telling. Good chance he'll ignore my next question, though he promised to answer me before. Still, I have to try.

"Am I?"

"Are you what?"

I swallow roughly. "Meant to be his?"

To my surprise, the answer comes quick. "No."

"How do you know? How can you be so sure?" A sinking suspicion hits me. "Am I meant to be with one of your kind? Is that why the Fae Queen is sending you people after me?"

Nine keeps his mouth clamped shut. He inhales through his nose, then exhales sharply. The word sounds like it's been dragged out of him when he finally whispers, "Yes."

And I know, because I've always been able to tell when someone's lying to me, that that *is* the truth.

Oh, boy.

I think I liked it a lot better when he didn't answer my questions.

I DON'T SLEEP AT ALL THAT NIGHT.

Even after Nine slips back into the shadows, vanishing from sight right before the sun comes up, I stay huddled in my bed. I'm too afraid to close my eyes now. What if I do and I'm transported back to the empty room where I danced with Rys?

I wait until my wake-up call that morning to throw open the door and plead with Amy to get me in to see whatever doctor is free.

Nine isn't real. Rys isn't real. I can't let them be. My life's so much easier when there's no such thing as the fae, and I spent the last few hours reminding myself of that. There has to be a reason why, after all this time,

I've had three separate episodes back-to-back. Sometime this morning, after the sun came up and I was still searching shadows for a figment of my imagination, I finally remembered my nighttime meds.

This all started on Sunday night, when I first could have sworn that I heard Nine's voice calling my name. Know what else happened on Sunday? I met Dr. Gillespie and he put in an order for a new medication.

That pink pill. Whatever the hell that thing is, it's not working.

I need a med check.

Just my luck, though. The first available doctor? Dr. Gillespie.

Because of course.

I almost have to laugh. Running on no sleep, as anxious as I am, I would rather talk to anybody else in Black Pine before Dr. Gillespie. And, sure, it's been a few days since our disastrous last session on Monday, but hell if I've forgotten how I told him all about Nine. The last thing I want to do right now is admit that I imagined a full-blown conversation with Nine for the first time in years.

I can hear the doctor now. He'll either say that I'm relapsing—again, tell me something I don't know—or that this is a breakthrough. Knowing how these psychologists all work, most likely he'll decide that it's because I opened up to him about Nine.

I hope not. I don't think I could sit there and look at the satisfied, smug expression on his impish face if he decides he's been here less than a week and he's already "fixed" me. Then again, if my verbal diarrhea our last session is what brought on these recent episodes, maybe he'll be the one who gets in trouble for it.

Here's hoping. All I know is that it's Friday, I won't have another check-in with Lorraine until Monday, and any of the other doctors for our ward are all booked up until this afternoon at the earliest.

It has to be Dr. Gillespie.

———

"RILEY, IT'S GOOD TO SEE YOU AGAIN. HOW ARE you today?"

"I'm tired." So, so tired.

Dr. Gillespie nods knowingly. "Well, yes, that happens sometimes as the sedation wears off. Your body is rested, but it takes a couple of days for the serum to dissipate and the grogginess to fade away."

I sink deep in my seat. "You heard about that?"

Of course he has. And look, I wasn't even a little wrong when I thought I'd be forced to see him with a smug grin.

Damn it.

The doctor opens his portfolio, picks up his pen. "Why don't you tell me why you're here? It's not your day to see me for a session, and I don't have you down for a check-in. I squeezed you in, so I only have a few minutes before my next patient. If it's okay with you, let's get right to it."

Okay. Right to it. I can do that.

"I need a new med check."

"Why would you say that?"

Why not? "I don't think my pills are working anymore."

"Which ones? Because I'll be honest with you, Riley. They don't work if you don't take them like you're supposed to. Every dose, every day. It's the only way you're going to see improvement."

Is he serious? Great. Looks like Nurse Stanley might've stopped by, had a chat with the new doctor. I don't care. Keeping my features neutral, I refuse to give away the truth on my face. I'm not kidding. And I didn't come to his office because I wanted a lecture.

I need *help*.

"I take all of my pills," I lie. At least, I have been the last few nights. "Every day, at the nursing station in the morning, then when a nurse and a tech bring me my pills at night. I don't want to see these hallucinations, you know."

"Mm-hmm."

Jeez, I would *love* to slap that stupid, smarmy grin right off his face. At this moment, if the asylum staff could assure me that I'd actually *be* alone, the solitary confinement to my room would so be worth it.

"Look, I'm telling you the truth. They don't work anymore." I grit my teeth and clench my fists, my leather gloves groaning in protest. I have to make him understand. "I don't know what else to say. You order a new pill for my nighttime cup and, ever since then, Nine's been back. I want him to go away."

That's all I had to say.

"You've seen him again?" Shoving the portfolio away from him, Dr. Gillespie leans forward in his seat, palms flush against the desktop. His big, blue eyes widen in abject surprise. "When? Where did you see him? Did he say anything to you?"

I'm taken aback by his reaction. I shimmy in my seat, climbing up so that I'm sitting straight. If he keeps acting weird, I'm ready to bolt out of here.

"Why do you care?" I ask him suspiciously. Then, because I can't help myself, I add, "You probably don't even believe me."

The doctor clears his throat. He leans back, a different kind of smile stretching his thin lips. "I'm your psychologist, Riley. I *have* to believe you." Dr. Gillespie pushes his glasses up his nose before pulling his portfolio—and my file—back toward him. He picks his pen up again. "Now," he says, "some questions about your... your friend. Did you hear him speak to you at all?"

"A little," I tell him. "But I... I don't remember what he said."

Because there's no way that I heard him tell me that Madelaine's killer thinks he's in love with me. Right?

Right.

"What about your vision? Did you actually see him?"

I shrug. "I don't know. I might have. The room was dark."

And Nine is a Dark Fae.

Shit.

"This didn't happen until I started taking that little pink pill the other day. It's not working. Please." I'll beg if I have to. Anything's better than going back to the old, familiar paranoia, expecting the fae to find me at any given moment. "You've got to do something to help me."

Dr. Gillespie opens my file, gesturing at something on the top page. "This says your medication has been changed multiple times over the last year. Something to do with a dependence on—"

"My blue pill."

"Right. According to Dr. Waylon's report, though, it seems to be the only prescription that ever helped you." He's quiet for a moment before he starts scribbling away on a page in his portfolio. "I'll keep your current dose as it is, but I'll add your old medicine to the order. We'll track your progress over the next couple of days and then we'll go from there. How does that sound?"

"Anything that'll work," I say honestly. I can hear the relief in my voice and don't even bother to disguise it. "Thank you so much."

"I want you to promise me something, Riley."

Right now I'm so glad that Dr. Gillespie is willing to do something to help me—whether he's humoring me or not—that I'd promise him my firstborn kid. Whatever he wants, he can have it.

"Anything."

"If you see Nine again, listen to everything he says. Remember it. Write it down if you have to. I'll get you some paper to keep by your bed, make sure the techs know it's approved. You're getting close, Riley, and you're running out of time. It's important that we get this straightened out. Keep notes and then come see me as soon as you can. I'll help you make sense of it all."

I nod. That's something I can do. I just hope that, once I start taking my blue pill again, I won't have to.

CHAPTER 10

I decide to chance eating dinner with the rest of the group tonight. If I get stuck with another nurse watching me like a hawk while I choke down dried-out chicken and watery jello for another night, they might actually have to restrain me this time.

I think Amy feels sorry for me. She hangs out past six when her shift is over, talking with Kelsey, one of the nighttime techs who takes over for the girls when Amy and Penelope are off. I don't know what she says, but I'm not rushed to my room when they lead us to the common room to eat, so that's something.

Dinner is beef stew with biscuits on the side. Comfort food. It tastes even better knowing that I'm eating it out in the open instead of in my room.

And it's not like I missed spending time with the other guys in my group. I didn't. Most of them are still watching me closely, waiting for me to pull a trick out of my gloves or something. I'll be the talk of the ward until someone else is more interesting than me.

Lovely.

It's better than going back to my room early, though. A lump forms in my throat every time I think of being locked inside, with its corner and the too-dark shadows that linger there.

Dr. Gillespie promised he'd fix my dose. I have to believe that it's going to work because, if I don't, it's way too easy to fall into old habits. Part of me wants to believe that Nine's back—even if he's returned with dire warnings that I'm willfully ignoring—while the rest of me just wants the fae to go away for once and for all.

Could I give up Nine to be sure that I never have to deal with the golden fae again?

In a heartbeat.

My reaction to his sudden reappearance last night was too weird. It's one thing to have an affection for the Shadow Man who helped me through my lost and lonely childhood. And, sure, you could say that I felt some sort of affection for him when I saw him again. Affection and a super strong attraction that scares me almost more than the idea that Rys is real, he's gunning for me, and I can't escape.

Dance with me.

Stay with me.

I'll always come for you.

I cough, choking on a lump of carrot that goes down

wrong. Tears well in my eyes as I swallow roughly before taking in great, big gulps of air.

Yeah. *Almost*.

I see Kelsey start toward me, then pause when I get myself under control. No one tries to slap me on my back or make sure that I'm okay. Smart. Who knows how I'd react if they touched me, even if they're trying to stop me from choking?

My throat burns. I take a couple of sips of water. It helps.

I know I'm dragging my heels, taking forever to eat my meal. I have this feeling deep inside that I shouldn't go back to my room. Something's coming. Something's going to happen. It's a hunch. A twisted premonition.

Jeez, I really hope my blue pill does what it's supposed to tonight.

The table begins to empty around me. I wonder if I could ask one of the techs if there are any extra biscuits. For the first time today, my stomach is settled. I've been feeling queasy ever since I woke up following the sedation. The comfort food is helping. I'd eat more if I could.

As if she can sense my hunger, Carolina rises from her seat. She picks up her bowl of stew, her biscuit—both obviously untouched—and moves around the table. That catches my attention. The garbage is on the other side of the room. Why is she coming this way?

She's wearing this crooked, hopeful little half smile on her too-thin face. Her dark eyes seem more sunken in than they usually do, purple bruises underlining them. She glances at me, then her gaze darts away. Like she's looking for someone—or she's desperate to avoid being caught doing something she's not supposed to.

Carolina's twitchy, too. Nibbling on a bottom lip that's so dry and cracked, it's gotta hurt like hell, she stops when she's about a foot away from me. She jumps in place when I look up at her. Her stew sloshes against the side of her bowl, splashing on the table, my arm, and the side of my glove.

"Oh, no! I'm sorry... I didn't mean to—"

"It's fine," I tell her.

"Let me clean it up."

With shaky hands, she sets the bowl down, the biscuit right next to it; the biscuit is partially wrapped in a napkin. Carolina grabs another napkin, eager to clean up her mess.

I move my hand out of her reach before she could dab at the spill on my glove. "I said, it's *fine*."

"Oh. Sure." Carolina gulps, then gives one last swipe with her napkin. "I... I really am sorry."

"Accidents happen. Don't worry about it."

"Here." She pushes her biscuit toward me. "You looked like you enjoyed yours. I thought you might want mine."

We'll both get in trouble if any of the techs notice that she's giving me her food—and that I'm taking it. Better get rid of the evidence. Mumbling a quiet thank you, I snatch the biscuit and take a huge bite before Kelsey or Frankie see me at it. Chew. Swallow. I do it again.

And that's when I notice the black smudge where the biscuit sat on Carolina's napkin. The biscuit is buttery, and it left a ring-shaped grease stain that caused the ink to run and turn blurry. Because, when I squint and look closer, I realize that's what the black smudge is.

It's writing.

Someone wrote four tiny lines on the napkin and covered it with a biscuit.

Setting the half-eaten biscuit on my plate, I pick up the napkin and squint to make out the words:

Find me after dinner.
We have to talk.
Tell no one else.
She has eyes everywhere.

I read it twice. It's not so blurry that I'm reading it wrong. But what the hell does *that* mean?

Lifting my head up, I start to ask Carolina. She's gone, though. While I was reading her note, she picked up her bowl and scurried away from the table. I watch as she dodges Kelsey, waiting until the techs are busy to get rid of her dinner.

Once she does, she turns back to look at our empty table. I'm the only one still sitting here so even if I could pretend she didn't mean for me to find this note, that disappears when our eyes meet.

I recognize that look. Carolina is lost, she's confused, and she's reaching out. I've got no fucking clue why she picked *me* of all people, but I've been where she is. She needs help.

Too bad I can't even help myself half of the time.

─────────

WITH CAROLINA'S NAPKIN CRUMPLED UP AND hidden in my fist, I go to my room after dinner because that's what I'm supposed to do. It's routine. Besides, it's not like I don't know that the techs and the nurses are keeping a closer eye on me than usual these last couple of days.

Part of me wonders if Dr. Gillespie put them up to it, or maybe Lorraine—my social worker is trying to do everything she can to make sure I'm released on time and, as much as I hate to admit, my breakdown the other night didn't do me any favors. Could be that they're all still on guard because they're expecting a repeat performance.

Regardless, I decide to wait until after I take my nighttime meds to see if I can sneak out to see Carolina. Lockdown isn't for another two hours. It might not be something I usually do—or, well, have *ever* done—but I can go visit another patient in my ward until lights out.

Ignoring Carolina's note isn't even an option. I have to know what she's talking about. Normally, I wouldn't give a shit. We all have our issues. There are countless professionals inside of Black Pine who are qualified to help her. Me? What can I do?

Nothing, that's what. Doesn't matter, though. It's the last line that got to me. *She has eyes everywhere...* She? Who the hell is *she*? It's bad enough that I've got Nine's warning about Rys and the other fae running around in my head. Am I supposed to be worrying about a *she* now?

Only one way to find out.

It's Friday night which means—thank God—no Nurse Stanley. No Duncan, either. He's been out since the night I lost my shit with Diana. A rumor has been circulating on our floor that the *crunch* I heard that night was the sound of my kick breaking Duncan's nose. Oops.

Whatever the reason, it's Frankie who comes with Nurse Pritchard tonight. I actually like this nurse. She's the oldest nurse in the ward, with thick, white curly hair that looks like there's a baby sheep sitting on her head. I don't see her very often, only when Nurse Stanley is having a night off, but she always smiles as if she's glad to see me.

She wears glasses that are half an inch thick and still squints through them. I used to practice fake-taking my meds with Nurse Pritchard before I was confident I would fool Nurse Stanley.

I'm not gonna need those skills tonight.

Her hands are shaky as she holds out my dixie cup. Careful to avoid her fingers, I grab the cup before she spills the pills onto the floor. I don't really want to take meds that hit the ground but, desperate as I am right about now, not gonna lie—I'd take them if they landed in a toilet.

Four pills line the bottom: my recent dose, plus my blue pill. I send a silent thank you to Dr. Gillespie as I toss the pills back. The water helps them go down easy.

Like Nurse Stanley, Nurse Pritchard expects me to open my mouth and show her that it's empty inside. Unlike Nurse Stanley, Nurse Pritchard seems satisfied that my pills are gone.

She should. Considering what happened last night, no way I'm missing this dose.

Frankie is built like Duncan, big and bulky, but that's the only similarity I can see. For one thing, Frankie is olive-toned, straight Italian, and Duncan is black. Duncan's bald head gleams like an eight-ball while Frankie has this thick, greasy black hair that he wears slicked back. Duncan always glowers. Frankie is a chatterbox. Now that I'm acting like a model patient, he chitchats while Nurse Pritchard takes my vitals and administers my medication.

I'm half listening to him. I give one-word answers when he pauses to take a breath. I guess it's enough. It's not like the techs expect that much from me anyway.

When they're done, Frankie helps Nurse Pritchard leave my room. He closes the door behind them, but it's not locked. Not yet. I can go track down Carolina as soon as I'm ready to.

Even though I'm anxious to see her, to find out what her cryptic note means, I'm not in a rush to leave.

I decide to stick it out in my room for a few minutes, give Frankie and Nurse Pritchard some time to move on to the next patient. I know Emma next door gets her meds brought to her room, too, as well as Tai in the guys' section of our floor.

The last thing I need is to draw attention from the facility staff because I'm acting out of the ordinary. I haven't spent the evenings outside of my bedroom since my first year inside of Black Pine and Dr. McNeil discovered I was talking to the shadows in the common room. As soon as I think it's emptied out a bit, I'll go see Carolina.

It's probably not the best idea, but I go and lay down on my bed. I'm not ready to go to sleep yet. I'm still wearing my hoodie—I'll take that off after I get back—and I traded my sneakers for my slippers; since I've given up on hiding my pills, I'm back to wearing my slippers before I go to bed. If anyone asks what I'm doing out of my room, I'm sure I can come up with something later.

I'm exhausted, though. Thanks to last night's hallucination, I haven't slept in more than twenty-four hours. My body is rundown. I feel achy and drained. Add that to my heavy dinner, and it's already a struggle for me to keep my eyes open. My mouth stretches wide as I try to fight a yawn.

I really want to see what's going on with Carolina. I *do*. But maybe I'll be able to make more sense out of this strange situation if I just rest my eyes for a couple of seconds.

I FALL ASLEEP BECAUSE OF COURSE I DO.

I'm only human.

It's not for long, though. An hour? If that. It's barely a refresher and, honestly, I feel worse for my short catnap. I've got this terrible taste in my mouth and I wish I'd left some of my water from my dixie cup to rinse it out. Ugh.

Something woke me up. I didn't mean to fall asleep in the first place, but as soon as I resurface, I realize exactly what cut into my rest.

The hum starts out low before it turns into an insistent buzz. I crack my eyes open in time for me to notice that one of the fluorescent light bulbs over my bed is starting to go bad. It flickers on and off, the hum growing even louder whenever it turns dark. Since it's still on, I know it's not past lights out time yet, and I'm wondering if I should go see if I can find Carolina now.

And that's when I hear his voice.

"Riley."

Oh, come *on*. I took my blue pill. It's why I went to see Dr. Gillespie this morning and begged for a med check. My pride was worth it. I didn't want to have to deal with Nine coming to see me again. I would've done anything to make it all go away.

Obviously, Nine didn't get the memo.

It's weird. I'm not used to seeing him unless it's super late and super dark. The flickering light doesn't do much to hide how hot he is.

Damn it. You'd think I would've toned down his ridiculous good looks the next time I conjured him since I'm so desperate to get rid of him. Seriously? Why does he have to be so gorgeous?

Though, as I get a better look at him in the dying light, I notice that he's a little bit different after all. I didn't think it was possible, but his skin has gotten even paler. His silver eyes seem duller than they did, the dark circles underneath a blemish on his otherwise perfect face. He's still wearing the same, strange, coat —it's like a leather duster but... but *not*—and it's not sitting right. It's kinda askew, one shoulder dipped lower than the other, his wavy hair trapped beneath it as if he threw it on in a hurry.

Still, no denying he's Nine. And he's in my room.

Again.

I sigh. Really? It's the only thing I can do right now. Anger and denial didn't do shit last night. I guess I'm up to barely masked frustration.

"You've got to be kidding me. What part of *you're not real, leave me alone* didn't you get?"

The Nine I knew from my childhood would've threatened to leave if I was so disrespectful. Not this Nine. Not the new, updated version of the Shadow Man.

This one just lets out a soft exhale. "You're still here."

Why does he sound so relieved? Where does he think I could've gone? "Well, yeah. But I'm supposed to be here." Then, in case he's forgotten, I add, "You're not. Why did you come back?"

"I wasn't sure if I'd be able to make it in time. I had to wait for the shadows to return to get to you and I thought, by then, I would've just missed you."

I can't help myself. I wave at the window. "Hello? Bars." I turn so that I can wiggle my fingers at the closed door. "Fully staffed facility. I've been locked in here for years. I'm not getting out for a couple of weeks. I'm not going anywhere."

"It might not be your choice."

His harsh words send a shiver up and down my spine. I don't like the way he said that. "What's that supposed to mean?"

"Did you forget everything I told you last night?" Nine clicks his tongue in annoyance. "I expect more from you than that."

Hallucination or not… figment of my imagination or a real-life fucking fae, I don't really care. At that moment, all I can think about is the Shadow Man I used to know and how I spent most of my life constantly searching for his approval. One kind word from Nine would have me floating with happiness for days.

A flippant or, worse, callous comment? It was like being slapped in the face.

I used to cry whenever I disappointed Nine. I used to pout whenever he treated me so coldly.

Now?

I'm just *angry*.

"Don't talk to me like that," I snap, sitting up so that I can glare over at him. "Don't know if you've figured it out yet or not, but I'm not a little girl anymore."

His silver eyes flash, reflecting the fluorescent light as it continues to whine and flicker. "Believe me, Shadow. I certainly noticed that."

Another shiver. The way he looks at me right now? I don't need my weird talent at being a human lie detector to know that he's telling the truth.

And I like it. I like the spark of interest way more than I should. Harboring this strange attraction to Nine is wrong in so many ways. I thought I was over my crush when he abandoned me shortly after Madelaine's death. I almost believed that I'd be happy if I never saw him again.

Having him so close, having him within arm's reach should I absolutely lose the rest of my sanity and actually *touch* him... I realize that I've been fooling myself all along. I might change my mind come morning, but now? Just like I couldn't accept that the golden fae was a hallucination even as I was dancing with him in my dreams, I know that Nine is real.

He's always been real.

Which means—

Panic begins to creep in. Blood drums in my ear, my breath picking up as I try to get air in quicker than I need to. The room starts to spin and I twist so that I'm about to climb out of my bed, slippers flat to the floor as I grip the edge of my mattress with gloved fingers.

Okay. *Okay*. I just need my meds to kick in. The blue pill will work. It's always worked before. It will work and then I'll be drifting away, leaving Nine behind as another nightmare.

Maybe if I keep on pretending, it'll finally come true.

"You're not real. You're *not*. You're a hallucination, Nine. I see you. I hear you. But you're not real."

"Ah, Shadow..." Nine leans forward. He doesn't leave the shadows in the corner, but I can tell from the dark expression that flitters across his face that he... he wants to. "I know this is a lot. You spent too long inside this place. It served its purpose, it kept you safe, but it went too far. I wanted you to be hidden from those who long to hurt you. I never expected you to forget all about them." He pauses. "About me."

"I've never forgotten," I say truthfully. "How can I? When, every morning, I have to confront that I'm here because I told the world that a fae killed my sister? I can't forget, but that doesn't mean this is really happening."

Nine spits out a word. Another one of those foreign words.

I try to echo it. "Ash-lynn? What?"

"He agreed that this was the only option I had. The asylum. It might have kept you alive, but at what cost?"

So this Ash-lynn person is a guy. It's not the golden fae—Nine called him Rys—which means there's another one out there who knows about me.

Great. Just great.

"Who the hell is Ash-lynn?"

"I can't explain. Not yet. Not now." Nine shakes his head when I start to argue. "Later, Riley. I swear it. But not now. Now, we have to go." He holds out his hand. "Come with me."

And… we're back to that again.

"I can't leave the asylum. I'm not like you. I can't just disappear."

"That's what you think."

"Nine—"

"You can leave this place any time you want to," he tells me.

And then he drops the bomb:

"How else are you visiting the cemetery?"

CHAPTER 11

How does he know that? *Nobody* knows that. Apart from drawing her stone angel during art therapy, I never share my sister with anyone in here unless I'm forced to during sessions.

Hell, even I've spent the last few years believing that my nighttime visits to Madelaine's graves are just really, really vivid dreams. Rain-soaked bangs? Sweat. Mud on my slipper? I must have stepped in something in the common room. I made excuses for it all because I *had* to. Anything else was impossible.

"How do you know that?" I demand.

Nine arches one midnight black eyebrow. It's a dark slash in his pale face as he says, "Do you deny it?"

"They're just dreams."

"For some, perhaps. But not for a shade-walker."

"A *what*?"

"It's a gift. A fae blessing. A shade-walker has the

power to travel through shadows," Nine explains. "You can go wherever you want, whenever you want."

"I'm not a shade-walker."

"You are."

He's telling the truth. But this is… this is *insane*. And that's saying something, coming from someone like me.

"Really? I've wanted out of here for close to six years now," I scoff. "I'm still here."

"Oh? That's probably because you've never tried before."

He's got me there. I can honestly say that I've never seen a shadow and thought, *Hey, I can travel through that.*

Nine is serious. I can tell. He's wearing the same expression he always used to wear whenever he told me stories about Faerie. Like he's teaching me something that I need to know and—oh, shit, I'm not supposed to be buying into any of this.

"Shade-walking is easier to do when you're sleeping. Your conscious mind will fight against what it deems impossible but, unconscious, there are no limitations to what you can do. Explains your graveside visits. With a little practice, you can control the shadows. It's a Dark Fae gift. I can teach you how to use it."

"Wait— *wait*. I'm not saying I believe any of this, but if I do? How do I have this gift?" A horrible suspicion hits me. "I'm… I'm not a Dark Fae or something, am I?"

Nine scowls at the same time as I realize that my horrified expression probably just insulted him. "No, you're not. It's a Dark Fae gift, but some are just born with it. In your case, you were—it's what drew you to the Fae Queen's attention. No changing it now. It's time for you to use that. If anything happens to me, it might be the only thing that can save you."

I ignore that part. The fae have been chasing me for more than twenty years according to Nine. They can wait five more minutes while I wrap my head around this whole shade-walking thing.

And it's not like I *want* to believe him—I don't—but there have been too many mornings where I woke up exhausted with dirty slippers and the smell of grave-yard soil in my nose.

"Okay," I admit. "Fine. So I visit the cemetery in my dreams. But I always wake up here. I'm not really going anywhere."

"Yes, Riley, you are. You have to understand. You come back to this place because it was safe. This asylum took over as your protector while I kept you shielded. But that time is over with. I'm here to take my job back." Nine extends his arm. "Come to me. Give me your hand."

It's the one thing I can't do. Not even for Nine. Too many years being taught that I should never, ever will-ingly touch a fae makes me refuse. Now that I know he's one of them, it's not even a question.

"I can't."

"You can," argues Nine with a frustrated sigh, "but you won't."

I shrug. "Call it what you want. I'm not gonna let you anywhere near me. Sorry."

"Very well. Then I'll just have to do it myself."

What? *No.* "You're not allowed. You need my permission. You can't—"

The creak of my doorknob turning cuts through the room, interrupting my frantic shouts. I clench my jaw shut, clamping my teeth together because, if I don't, I'll start screaming. I know I will. And the last thing I need is to be sedated again.

Frankie peeks his head inside of my room. The fluorescent light bulb continues to flicker, the light bouncing off of his oily hair. I only realize how loud the hum has gotten when Frankie glances up at it in confusion.

I use those two seconds to steal a look at the corner.

As sudden as he arrived, Nine is gone. Good. I don't know what would have been worse: explaining Nine to Frankie if the big tech saw him, or dealing with reality when it turned out that Frankie couldn't.

He points up at the dying bulb. "This just go out?"

I can't speak yet. My heart is lodged in my throat, thumping away like mad. Okay. I was wrong. The absolute *last* thing I needed right now is to deal with one of the techs walking in on me while I'm having a full-blown freak-out at Nine.

Who cares that the Shadow Man is gone? It actually makes it *worse.*

Gulping, trying to force back the lump inside my throat, I simply nod.

"I was coming to tell you that it's lights out. Gonna lock the doors in a few. You okay in here, Thorne?"

My mouth is dry. That was a direct question. I'm not so sure I can get away with nodding again. My voice is weak, a little shaky, as I try to come up with a reason why I look like I'm about to lose it. Frankie's not dumb. I see the furrow in his brow as he peers closely at me. He knows something is up.

I point at the light. "Just trying to figure out how to get it to stop doing that. It's kinda freaking me out, the way it keeps flickering like that. You don't think it's gonna blow, do you?"

He glances up at it in concern, as if the idea has occurred to him, too. "Better safe than sorry," he decides. "I'll go get maintenance."

"Oh. Really? Thanks."

"Hang tight. I'll be right back."

Frankie closes the door behind him when he leaves. There's not much time. I immediately scramble out of my bed, tiptoeing toward the door. There's a small, square window in the center. I peek out into the corridor.

Nurse Pritchard is standing near the nursing station, filing a chart. Kelsey is putting her coat on, ready to end her shift. Frankie is nowhere in sight.

"I don't like the way he was looking at you. He watched you too long."

At the sound of the lyrical voice with a harsh edge, I whirl around just as the fluorescent light finally gives out. It pops, the light dimming as the annoying humming whines to a stop. All I can hear now is my frightened breathing.

Nine moves like a cat. I mean it. I never see him come or go. He's just *there*. Where did he disappear to?

Even worse, why do I insist on bringing him back?

Squinting in the sudden darkness, I pick him out from the rest of the shadows. "I thought you were gone."

"I'm not going anywhere without you, especially now that I'm sure the asylum has been compromised. Someone has to protect you, Shadow. I gave my word. I must do this."

There's a threat in there that's impossible for me to ignore. I back up against the closed door, prepared to bang on it if he even so much as looks at me funny. "Stay back. You can't touch me. I won't let you."

"That's fine," Nine says solemnly. Then, for the first time tonight, he steps out of the pitch-dark shadows in the corner. The air shifts and I know—I just... I just *know*—that Nine is actually here with me. Not in the same room, not tucked in the shadows, but within touching reach. He's really, really here. And then he tells me, "I don't have to have your permission for this."

"For what? I don't understand— "

"There's no time. He'll be back."

"Nine, what are you— *no!*"

He grabs my arm in a grip so tight that I can already imagine the bruise that will be there in the morning. I try to jerk out of his grip, but it's impossible. He yanks my arm and, suddenly, the room starts spinning like I've gotten tossed inside of a tornado.

I open my mouth to scream but the sound gets lost in the rush of air. My hair starts whipping around me, the white-blonde strands mingling with Nine's raven-colored waves. Dark mixed with light. Black and white.

Ha. As if it was that simple.

Everything blurs. Wind whooshes through me, an angry breeze that slaps me with the ends of my hair, my cheeks rippling at the force of it. It's a chilly burst of air that freezes the tips of my ears. They've always been super sensitive and it's been so damn long since I felt the wind on my skin like that.

It doesn't last long and by the time my teeth are chattering from the chill, a suppressing heat slams into me. I choke, then gag. That's probably not because of the temperature change. The spinning is making my already queasy stomach violent.

I used to get car sick when I was a kid. This is ten times worse.

I clamp my eyes closed, screwing my jaw shut so that I don't throw up my beef stew all over Nine's shadowy coat. He might deserve it for what he's doing right now, but I'd only regret it in the end.

My whole body jerks, like when you're riding on a train and it stops short. If Nine wasn't gripping my arm so tight, I would've gone flying when the world seems to just… stop.

Once I'm standing still, once I'm sure the world has

stopped spinning, I crack my eyelids open—and immediately wish that I *didn't*.

My first thought is that I probably should've paid closer attention to what the nurse stuck in my dixie cup because one of those pills has got to be wrong. I'm tripping pretty hard on something. That's the only way I can explain what I'm seeing.

The sky is this freaky pink. Not a soft pale color, either, but a dark magenta mixed with large swirls of a deep, burnished gold. I don't see any sun or stars or even clouds. Just a purply-pink sky.

The trees are even worse. I mean, they're beautiful —but they look like they're made of crystals. If it wasn't for the heat here, or the fact that it's still June, I'd think they were bare trees with a silver bark, empty branches dripping with icicles. I don't know how else to explain their sparkle and shine.

The air is thin here, or maybe I've forgotten how to breathe. I bend over with my gloves on my knees and look at what *should* be the grass. It looks like spun sugar or dental floss or, well, anything but grass. Because in the real world? Grass isn't this shade of a pretty light blue.

Hunched over, torn between running my fingers through the weirdo grass and flipping out because it's starting to hit me that I'm not in the real world anymore, I finally notice that Nine isn't holding onto my arm.

For one horrible second, I think that I lost him in the whipping wind, but then I turn around and he's looming behind me. From the look on his gorgeous face, I'm betting he didn't expect to be in this strange place anymore than I do.

He catches my eye. Without a word, he puts one long, pale finger to his lips. There's a shiny patch of raw skin along the side of his finger and most of his hand.

I've seen marks like those before. Nine has a freshly healed burn.

"Where are we?" I whisper. And then, because indignation can only protect me so much and I'm two seconds away from shaking in my slippers, I hiss, "So I know I haven't been on the outside in a while, but I think I would've remembered if the sky was *pink*."

Nine ignores my question. "Just stay close to me. We went a few portals too far. We shouldn't be here. I'll give you a couple of seconds to recover, then we'll try again."

Is that a threat? Now that I'm standing straight again, freaking out has won out and I'm way too busy to notice much of anything else. I force myself to pay attention to Nine. He's a fae, right? A Dark Fae who just proved we can both walk through shadows together. He knows what he's doing, right?

A couple of seconds, then we're getting the hell out of here. Okay. That calms me a little.

I still don't know exactly what this place is. I start turning in circles, marveling at its strange, undeniable beauty when, suddenly, I glimpse someone in the distance, halfway hidden behind one of the trees. I jump back. From his whisper, it's obvious Nine doesn't want anyone else to know we've popped in. Crap. That's definitely a person over there.

I blink. Wait a second. That's... that's a *person*. Not a fae. His skin is a light brown shade—not bronzed, not moonlight pale—and, even from where I am, I can tell that he's shorter than Nine. He's still tall, though. And there's something about him that's... that's *familiar*. Squinting, I look closer.

No fucking way.

Nine is hanging back. The Shadow Man's gotta be proud of himself. He got what he wanted. I'm here, wherever here is, and I'm not screaming my head off.

Yeah. That's about to change.

Before he can stop me, I bolt. I have to be sure that I'm right. I don't know how it's possible, but I have this absolutely awful suspicion about the guy tucked behind that weirdo tree over there. Who knows? Maybe I'm deflecting. I don't want to deal with Nine so why not run off into this unknown place?

"Riley," he hisses after me. "No!"

I ignore Nine. He's bigger than me, and probably faster, but I want it more. I pull up to the tree seconds before I sense Nine closing in on me from behind. That's more than enough time for me to prove that I wasn't seeing things.

It's Jason. And he isn't moving.

Still as a statue, his big, black eyes wide but unseeing, he has one hand held out in front of him as if he was begging before he was frozen in place. The wispy, floaty candy floss that's supposed to be grass is creeping up his legs, wrapping around his knees. He's trapped.

I've got to get the hell out of here before that happens to me next.

I back into Nine, hitting his chest with my shoulder in a frantic attempt to escape the terrible truth in front of me. I bounce off of him, my hoodie and his jacket protecting me from another touch. He reaches for me. I dodge him easily, my gloved fingers trembling as I press them to my lips.

Jason. The goofy, smiling, optimistic guy from Black Pine. He always seemed nice, and he spent countless sessions detailing the big plans he had for what his life was going to be like when they finally let him back out.

He's been gone from the asylum the last few days. I remember missing him at breakfast… what day was that? Sunday. Pancakes. He wasn't there. He was missing.

No.

Not missing.

He's in Faerie. With a certainty that I can't explain, I know that's where he is.

And, now, so I am.

CHAPTER 12

"**W**hat happened to him?" The words slip out through the gaps between my fingers. I'm shaking. "What happened to Jason?"

Nine makes a rough sound in the back of his throat. Not a scoff, or a huff. It's frustration mixed with fury and, despite my shock at seeing Jason like that, I can tell Nine's not mad at me.

But hell if he isn't angry.

"You know that human?" he asks.

I nod.

"Then he's a warning to you."

What? "I don't—*what*? What do you mean, a warning?"

"The Fae Queen. These are her gardens. She would've left him here for you to find him if you came to Faerie before she had you brought to her." Nine's silver eyes don't seem so out of place in this otherworld. They shine in his face, a perfect match to the bark on the tree that shadows Jason. "He was in the asylum."

It's not a question. I nod anyway.

"How long?"

I swallow roughly. "I don't know. A year maybe? Two. I didn't really pay attention. He was nice, though. He doesn't deserve this."

"If he's here, then you can be sure the human deserves a fate far worse than this," Nine says coldly.

The iciness in his voice stings me. I flinch, then step away from him, balling my hand into a fist and dropping it at my side. "How can you be so heartless?"

"I'm not. My loyalty is to only one who has human blood." Me. He's talking about me. "Besides, he was as good as dead the first time he let Melisandre touch his soul. He belonged to the queen. To leave him in her garden as a statue is a kindness compared to what I would have done to the mortal if I discovered he was working against you."

"Jason?" I turn to look at the statue again, trembling noticeably when it's pretty damn obvious that he really *is* a statue. He hasn't moved an inch. "He wasn't working against me. I barely knew the guy. He was just another patient inside—"

"No. He wasn't." Nine glides easily around me, blocking Jason from my sight. "Don't you understand? I needed you safe. I needed to put you somewhere protected before the Fae Queen sent her soldiers after you. But she did anyway. Not fae—you would've sensed them in your domain the second they crossed into the human world. But another human? You'd never guess they were on the side of the queen."

"I don't get it. Why would he work for her?"

"Not just that human," Nine admits. "As soon as I discovered that they knew where to find you, I took the first portal to the asylum. It wasn't just the male. I could sense more than a few touched humans inside that place. It's why I knew I had to get you out of there before any of your enemies got to you first."

I immediately think of Diana, the blonde tech whose eyes flashed golden the other night. Of how uncomfortable she made me. What about Dr. Gillespie? He was always way too interested in Nine. How many times did I think it was super weird how my psychologist was humoring me by acting like my hallucinations were real?

Too many, but it made sense if *he* knew that they weren't hallucinations at all.

He's telling the truth. As painful as it is—as incredibly unbelievable as it is—Nine is telling the truth.

"Why?" I forget in the heat of the moment that Nine wanted me to be quiet. The word bursts out of me with all the subtlety of a bomb going off. I'm an almost twenty-one-year-old orphan. I'm not supposed to have *enemies*. "What the hell does she want with me?"

"It's because you're the Shadow."

I'm not a statue, but I go still like one.

I know that voice. Lilting and lyric, it's deep enough

to belong to a man, and rich enough to make me want to turn around and see him—even though I know better.

When I manage to break my sudden spell of paralysis, I search for him.

There he is. Rys. The golden fae—the Light Fae—who killed my sister has joined us in the gardens.

In this strange place, he is absolutely brilliant. His lovely, bronze-colored skin is nearly a match for the swirls in the sky, his golden eyes flashing and reflecting the silver trees. He moves purposefully but easily, like he doesn't have a care in the world. Long, tawny hair drifts behind his lean body as he glides toward me.

His lips part. A whisper on the still breeze.

I have an irresistible urge to go to him—

"Riley," snaps Nine. "Stay strong. Fight it."

But I don't *want* to—

"Shadow," Nine says, more feeling in his harsh voice. "Stop moving!"

I jam the heels of my slipper into the fluffy, wispy, flossy grass. My shins strain as I fight the pull toward Rys. And it's not just because Nine told me to stop.

I want to stop.

I do. When about ten feet still separate me from him, I finally manage to put on the brakes. I'm panting at how much of my strength it took to fight the compulsion to go to him, but I stop.

"You've taken too many liberties, Rys." Nine moves so that he's standing beside me. He points at the Light fae. "I could sense your brand on her skin the second I returned to her. You touched her."

"And you've told her about the Shadow Prophecy before she came of age," Rys counters. "Seems we both did a little trickery."

"I did no such thing. I kept to the terms of my bargain."

"You called her Shadow."

"It's just another name for her. That's all."

"Ah, that's right. Because you don't know her true name." Rys turns to me, his eyes sparkling in delight. "We've shared more than a touch, you and I. Isn't that right?"

Whether I'm doing it to myself or he is, suddenly the song from the night I danced with him in my dreams is filtering in through my ears, beating against the back of my skull. I grit my teeth, desperate to ignore it.

I can't. Not only that, but my hands grow even hotter inside of my gloves. I can't forget how I let him touch me, the sizzle I felt when our bare skin connected, or how weak and drained I was as he sapped me of all my energy.

He touched me. And I *let* him.

I wrap my arms around me, hugging myself. Nine moves forward, shielding me with his body as he steps between Rys and me.

"You interfered," he accuses the other fae.

"You say interfere, I say that I'm just doing what I must to claim what's mine. I'm not like Melisandre.

The prophecy doesn't faze me, Nine. Riley's got enough blood in her to be a proper *ffrindau* for me. I want her. I've waited long enough to take her. Leave her with me and your debt is repaid. You can go."

Nine reaches into his pocket. Of all things, he pulls out a rock. Seriously. A rock. About the size of a nickel, he holds it up, then lets it nestle in his palm. He cradles it like its heavier than it appears. "You don't have the power to clear it."

Rys holds out his hand. "Then pass it to me. I'll gladly take it."

What are they talking about? I thought I was confused because I was still shaking off the woozy feeling that hits me every time Rys pulls that command shit on me. Nope. When Nine looks at the rock in his palm, before vanishing it into the depths of his coat again, I can honestly say I have no clue what the fuck is going on.

"A rock?" I blurt out. "What's so special about a *rock?*"

Rys grins. "It's a token of Nine's favor for a human."

Nine's entire expression closes off. "It was no favor, Rys. You know that. It was a command."

"From a human," Rys says again. His grin widens, turning almost predatory. "A mother's last command to protect her infant daughter." He traces his jaw with his slender, bronzed, pointer finger. "Though, I've often wondered, shouldn't her fate free you of any debt you feel obligated to repay? Yet still you linger about my mate, like an unwanted shadow."

His words are like an arrow to my chest. My whole body jolts as I realize with a sudden start that I'm the infant daughter Rys is talking about. The human? That's got to be my mother.

They're talking about my *mom*.

I whirl on Nine. "My mother asked you to protect me?"

"Commanded," corrects Rys cheekily.

I can't even look at him. Mate? That's gonna be a nope. Maybe if I hope real hard, he can join Jason in being a statue in this freaky garden.

Besides, my attention is super locked in on Nine. He knows it, too. His silver eyes have dimmed, the razor-sharp edge of his cheekbones jutting out as he sucks in a breath.

"My mother commanded you to protect me?" I ask him a second time. I wave behind me, gesturing where I think Rys is still standing. My hands are shaking. "What does he mean by debt? And her fate? What happened to my mom?"

"Yes, Nine. Answer her," Rys calls out. "You were at the gas station that day. You know."

I'm sure Nine can see the hope in my expression as I gaze up at him. Apart from the grainy, black and white footage from twenty years ago, this is the only thing I've ever heard about the woman who left me behind.

I long ago accepted that she'd done it on purpose.

Could it be that she had no choice?

"Do you?" I ask him. "Do you know what happened to her? To *me*?"

Nine glares past me. If looks could kill, the Light Fae would be six feet under this candy floss grass in a heartbeat. "I left her alone after the contract was made. I have no idea what happened to Callie after I returned to Faerie. Riley's my concern, not her human mother. And I've done everything to protect her, like I said I would."

I'm used to Nine's cold and callous attitude when it comes to humans. I've known for a long time that I'm the only exception when it comes to his outright disdain for anybody in the human world. I was so happy to have him care about me—even if it was in his stilted, limited way—that I never second-guessed him when he said he was sent to watch over me.

I had no fucking clue that he'd been *commanded* to.

This is a double gut punch. I learned two things just now. One? My mom's name is Callie. I tuck that deep inside, that small nugget of information that brings me closer to the woman I lost. And two? Nine only ever looked after me because someone forced him to.

I don't have my mom. I guess I never really had my Shadow Man, either.

"Is that why you visited me as a kid?" I ask him. "A… a debt?"

The fae can't lie, but I'm betting that Nine's wishing that he could because it takes him a few pointed seconds before he finally nods.

"Yes."

"She made you do it."

"Yes, but, Riley—"

Nope. That's all I needed to hear.

"I want to go back to the asylum," I say, interrupting him. "Take me back. Now."

"I can't." He says *can't*. I know from his demeanor that he means *won't*. Now I know where I got it from. "It's not the place for you any longer. You can't go back."

I whirl around, facing Rys. "You."

Rys arches one of his perfect eyebrows. His smile is playful. I hate him for that. "Yes, my *ffrindau*?"

Ffrindau. I know what Nine said that meant. soulmate. Yeah, right. That's never gonna happen, but I'm not above using this fae to get what I want. "Can you bring me back to the asylum?"

"I'll do anything you ask of me."

"She doesn't need you, Rys. She has me." Nine bristles, visibly annoyed. That's… that's new. He never used to let me see such an emotional reaction. Rys has obviously gotten to him.

"We can't go back to the asylum, Riley, but we don't have to stay here."

Nine's whole demeanor changes as he turns to me. It almost sounds like he's pleading—but why would a fae plead with a nobody human like me?

Then he says, "I'll take you somewhere else to keep you protected," and I remember.

That's right. Because of his debt.

Huh. No thanks.

Right now, I don't want either one of them. My shock's fading. Blood is rushing past my ears as my heart beats out of control. My vision is dimming; black spots are closing in on the corners. I'm on the verge of a monstrous panic attack. I take a couple of deep breaths in an attempt to calm myself. It's useless. It feels like something inside of me is clawing its way out. I gasp and pull on the collar of my hoodie, trying to get more out of this weak air before I lose it entirely and I can't go home at all.

Neither Nine nor Rys has noticed that I'm teetering on the edge. Nine is staring at the Light Fae. Rys is wearing a smirk that shouldn't be half as attractive as it is.

"If you take her, I'll just chase after her."

"You can't follow her in the shadows."

"No," Rys agrees. "But plenty of Melisandre's soldiers can."

I don't know who this Melisandre person they keep bringing up is, but I've got a pretty good guess. Who seems to have a reason to come after me *and* has access to soldiers? She's got to be the Fae Queen.

And we're currently in her gardens. While Nine and Rys bicker like children, I'm a sitting duck. Nine wanted me to be quiet? Yeah, that ship sailed a while ago.

I don't want to turn into a statue like Jason.

"Nine," I say, because if the choice is between my Shadow Man and the golden fae, I know who I'm sticking with, "let's just go. I don't care where. I can't stay here. It's too hard for me to breathe."

In an instant, Rys loses the last of his playful nature. He grows deadly serious and, in his golden eyes, I get a glimpse of the dangerous, capricious creature who snapped Madelaine's neck because he wanted to prove a point.

I choke on another gasp, throwing my hands up as I stumble back. Nine is slender, but he's tall. If I crouch a little, I can hide behind him.

The way Rys is looking at me all of a sudden, I *have* to.

"You will stay with me," he says in a booming voice at odds with its normally smooth and cajoling tone. It's an obvious command. I shiver and start to stand up straight, though there's nothing about his words that make me feel like I must.

I hesitate, keeping Nine between us.

Rys glowers. Hate fills his gaze as he glances at Nine before he turns to me. A mixture of lust and desire twists his expression until I know that there's no way I'm getting out of this without him trying to call me to him again.

I'm right.

"Come to me. Come, Zel—"

He never finishes his command.

Nine stiffens. I'm not so sure why—and his back is to me so I can't see his face—but I sense a change in him as soon as Rys starts to say that weird *Zella* word again. Before Rys can utter the second syllable, Nine's pale skin begins to glow.

He spares one glance at me, a quick peek to make sure I haven't moved, then he zeroes in on the Light Fae.

If Rys's shine is brilliant in this strange place, Nine's vibrant silver glow makes him absolutely terrifying. The fierce expression on his face isn't helping me, either. Holy shit. I've never been afraid of Nine before, but I guess there's a first time for everything because I'm about to flip the fuck out.

I gasp for another breath, certain that I'm about to just pass out already. Only the fact that I'm in Faerie—I'm in the Fae Queen's gardens—keeps me standing. I'm already super vulnerable. Fainting here?

Might as well just walk up to her castle and say hi while I'm at it.

While I struggle to hold it together, Nine lifts his hand again. After muttering something in that harsh, foreign language of his, he makes a gesture I don't understand. I can't really see it. Blackness is creeping up on the edge of my sight, though I wince and squint when he stretches his fingers. It's like he's turned a flashlight on. A bright silver beam shoots out at Rys, breaking up some of the fog that's clouding my vision.

It pushes the Light Fae back a few feet. The grin slides from Rys's face as he lifts one delicate hand to shield his gaze.

"You shouldn't have done that, Nine."

"Leave us," he orders. "You don't believe in the

Shadow Prophecy. I've dedicated too many years to it. The Shadow belongs to the Dark Fae. Accept it."

"Aislinn was a Light Fae," Rys counters. "My claim is stronger."

"Fate will win."

"Or perhaps the queen will."

No, I think as I allow myself to give in to the panic scrabbling against the last of my consciousness. It's been there since I first saw the magenta sky mixed with gold, the crystalline trees, Jason the statue. I'm light-headed and weak, the anxiety crashing into me like a wave. I don't fight it anymore.

At the moment, I decide that *Riley* will win.

I remember what Nine told me. When I'm conscious, I can't accept that I can do that shade-walking shit. But what if I'm *not* conscious?

There's no sun here—but there are shadows every-where. Lurking behind the unnatural, fantastical trees, like the one that's nearly hiding Jason, I see the shadows and, despite my cloudy, fuzzy head, I have to wonder.

It's worth a shot.

I start to fall, my eyes rolling into the back of my head. Every part of me locks up, my arms shrinking against my torso as I let myself go, aiming for the patch of hazy black that stretches across the ground.

I lock my jaw as I collapse. I refuse to give either of them permission to catch me before I hit the ground.

I only hope the weird grass is as soft as it looks.

CHAPTER 13

When I come to again, the first thing I look for is my window with its six bars across it.

Nope. No window. No bars. All I see is the night sky above my head and it hits me: I'm not at Black Pine anymore.

I'm not even *inside*.

A handful of stars twinkle in the distance, a few bright spots in the blackness above me. It takes a second before I understand that I'm lying on my back on the cold ground. Grass cushions me. I can feel it scratching me through my hoodie.

With a grunt, I roll onto my side. I blink a few times, trying to get my sight back, then use the dim moonlight to peer at the grass surrounding me.

It's pointy. Kinda brittle and dry, flat where my body pressed it into the dirt.

And, thank God, it's *green*.

I don't know where I am. Not quite yet. At least I can be sure of one thing, though: I'm not in the Fae Queen's gardens anymore.

"Riley. You're finally awake."

I'm not alone, either.

Nine is crouched beside me, his body low, the tail of his long jacket flaring out behind him. It flaps in the cool wind. It's not so warm here, not so humid, and when I tilt my head back so that I can look at the sky again, it's a relief to see that I'm back in the human world.

Lowering my gaze, I pull myself into a sitting position. I can feel the weight of his open stare and purposely avoid his eyes, his words, and his presence. I'm so stinking pissed at him, I want to knock him over. It would definitely be worth having to touch him.

I put my petty revenge on the back-burner when it finally clicks. I recognize the scene around me with a sudden jolt. Okay. Hold on. I know *exactly* where I am.

There's the gate, unlocked for the moment, though I know the caretaker's habits. At ten minutes to midnight, he'll start his final rounds before he locks up for the night. A couple of rows away from where I am, I see the Richardsons' mausoleum, the stone behemoth that shielded me from the rain the last time I was here.

And there, somewhere on the west side of the cemetery, I'll find the concrete angel that stands guard over Madelaine's grave.

It's like what Nine said. I could run through shadows while I'm awake and nothing would ever happen because, after six years of therapy and denials, it's too hard for me to believe in the impossible. When I let myself faint, though? I must've hit that shadow and my body brought me back where I belong.

Nine got in my head. I should've landed in my bed at Black Pine—it's where I've traveled every other time I, well, I sleepwalked through the shadows. All of his arguments about the asylum being compromised got to me. Self-preservation must've kicked in. I'm not in Black Pine.

I'm in Acorn Falls.

I don't know how much time has passed. It's late, the chilly temperature washing away the last of the evening's heat. Besides the fact that it's pitch-dark around me, Nine's presence is a pretty big clue that it's still night out. As soon as the sun's up again, he'll be gone.

I... I don't know how I feel about that yet.

I'm so used to ducking and hiding when I find myself suddenly in the cemetery. Especially now that I know I'm really *here*, I don't want the grizzled old care-taker to find me sitting on a plot, hanging out with a fae who can shoot laser beams out of his palm.

That totally happened. It all happened. Escaping the asylum, visiting the Fae Queen's gardens, finding Jason... confronting Rys. It all happened.

I wait for the panic to crash over me. It doesn't. I think I've been pushed way past my limit at this point. Like, I'm so spent, I'm looking at the impossible series of events from tonight and just shrugging them off. I mean, it can't get much worse, can it?

I'm glad I made it here. Just knowing that I'm hiding out in the Acorn Falls cemetery gives me a tiny bit of peace. Doesn't matter how I got here. It's night. Nine might be here, but Rys isn't. The Fae Queen isn't.

It's something.

I lean against the nearest gravestone. *Robin Maitland, 1912-1989*. She had a good, long life. *Treasured wife and mother*. She sounded nice. I don't think she'd mind me using her final resting place to take a breather.

The chill of the marble stone cuts right through the material of my hoodie.

Eh. It's not so bad. It could be raining.

The grass rustles, the swish of Nine's duster whispering in the wind as he gets to his feet. He moves so that he's standing in front of me. Without a word, he offers his bare hand out.

"I know you're kidding." I sound tired. So very tired. These small catnaps aren't doing enough for me to recharge. Slumping back on the grass, I lean against Robin Maitland's headstone. It's as much for support as it is to cover me from the caretaker's lantern. "Get back down. You don't want to get us caught."

He doesn't move. "I'm not worried about what a human can do to me."

No. Of course not.

"Yeah. Well, maybe I'm worried about what you'll do to a human. It's not the caretaker's fault we crashed here."

Nine blinks. His outstretched hand falls to slap the side of his thigh. "You'd want me to spare him? He's obviously a threat to you."

So I was right. Dark Fae or Light Fae, it doesn't matter. Just like Rys killed Madelaine as almost an afterthought, Nine wouldn't even think twice about offing the cemetery caretaker.

The fae might be beautiful, but they're also terrible.

"He's not a threat. He's an old man who takes care of the graves at night. I don't want any trouble."

Even as I say the words, I know it's pointless. Trouble? I'm already in it up to my ears.

"As you say, Shadow."

Shadow. I wince, closing my eyes. Did he really have to go there?

"Don't call me that."

"It's your name."

"*My* name is *Riley*."

"That's what your first human family called you. That's not your name."

My stomach drops to my slippers.

That's right. Not only has he hidden this prophecy thing from me but, holy shit, he actually *knew* my mother.

"So my mom named me Shadow?" I say warily. I wish I had more energy. I want to get up and pace, maybe even rant and scream and demand Nine tell me *everything*, but I'm too tired. I haven't gotten more than an hour or two of sleep in almost two days. Plus, my panic attacks always take every inch of my strength. I push on, though, because I have to. "Or do you call me that because of that stupid prophecy the other monster mentioned?"

"He's not a monster."

"Po-ta-to, po-tah-to. He's a killer."

Nine smartly stays quiet.

I grab a handful of the grass that covers Robin Maitland's grave. I won't touch him, but I'm frustrated enough to throw the blades at Nine. They flutter in the wind, covering the tip of his shiny boot.

He frowns. "Was that necessary?"

Yes. "Tell me about the Shadow Prophecy."

"What if the human finds you here?"

"You just said you'd spare him if I wanted you to. I want you to. It'll be fine. Now, stop stalling. I went with you to that weirdo place. I left Black Pine. Now it's your turn. What was he talking about? What's this prophecy and what the hell does it have to do with me?"

Throwing his coat behind him, Nine crouches down so that he's right beside me. His silver eyes beam in the darkness, brighter than the lantern the caretaker uses. He isn't blinking, watching every tired line on my face as I wait for him to answer.

I want to go to sleep, but I'm still shaken up from the scene with Rys. What if I do and he follows me into my dreams again? I can't risk it. Not yet.

"Tell me about the prophecy, Nine. Please."

Maybe it's the *please* that gets to him. I'll never

know. After nodding a few times, Nine begins to explain.

"There's an ancient prophecy in Faerie. Melisandre has been queen for almost two centuries and she has no plans on abdicating anytime soon. She's ruthless, Riley, and she's gone further than most to secure her crown. The lesser citizens call it the Reign of the Damned, though she takes tongues from those who say it."

I swallow reflexively. She cuts out tongues? Oh, shit. "Okay, well, she sounds like a peach. But what does this queen have to do with me?"

"It's the Shadow Prophecy. It's been said that a shade-walker—the Shadow—will have the power to defeat the Fae Queen. With Melisandre's death, the Reign of the Damned will come to an end. You can imagine that she's desperate to keep her head."

Tongues and heads. Good thing I still haven't eaten —my stomach lurches at the images he's sticking in my mind.

And that's not even the worst of it.

It takes me a minute to process what he just told me. I don't know what I was expecting him to say—but you can bet it wasn't that. I'm not like Rys. I'm not a murderer. I don't care what this stupid prophecy says. I'm not about to kill anyone—especially not the Fae Queen.

I'm just a broken human. How would someone like me go up against an all-powerful faerie queen in the first place?

"So what? I'm supposed to be this Shadow person because I can walk through shadows? You can do it, too. You said it was a Dark Fae gift."

"It is. The Shadow has human blood, though. It can't be a fae."

Oh. *Wonderful.* "Is it true?" I demand. "Am I the Shadow?"

"She believes you are," Nine mutters. "That's all that matters. She'll end your life before you get the chance to end hers. When you were a child, she wasn't so concerned. But now that you're coming of age…"

Coming of age. How much do I want to bet that, to the fae, that means twenty-one?

You've got to be kidding me. All of Nine's mentions of a villainous *she* start to pop up in my memories. After the golden fae—after Rys—asked me to dance that first time and he killed Madelaine when I refused to leave the Everetts with him, I forgot all about the *she* who was after me. I had a real monster, a male monster, that I spent years obsessing over.

I never knew that it was the Fae Queen who was really after me.

Gulping, I ask him, "And there's nothing I can do about it?"

"Not right now."

That's not a no. I know better than to push him, though. When I was a kid, Nine hated it when I asked him questions. He'd rather I sit and listen because, eventually, he would tell me everything he thought I needed to know. To have him answering my questions, treating me like an equal… I shouldn't be so impressed, but I am. So the bar hasn't been set all that high for me. I get it. He made me a promise because he wanted something I didn't want to give him. Now that I'm out of the asylum, he could decide that that bargain has been met.

I have to get more answers out of him before he shuts the conversation down. He'll do it. I've seen him.

Besides, there's nothing I can do about the queen right now. So she thinks she has to kill me because I want to kill her? I'll leave her alone if she doesn't bother me. That seems fair.

So what if I "come of age" in two weeks? As far as I'm concerned, being twenty-one means two things: I'm out of Black Pine and I can finally buy booze legally.

Committing regicide? Yeah. I'm good.

At least now I know why my mom would've turned to another fae to protect me. I still don't know how she is involved—how she knew Nine, or that the fae were real to begin with—but it makes sense. Nine is a cold bastard. If there was anyone I'd choose to be a protector, it would be him.

"You knew my mom."

Nine's expression goes blank. It wasn't a question, but he treats it like one. "We've met."

"That's what he said. I didn't want to believe him."

"Who? Rys?"

I can't bring myself to say his name. "Yeah. The Light Fae. He said she commanded you to watch over me. How? She's a human."

His eyes dim. "Do you believe him?"

That's not an answer. Is my Dark Fae trying to be tricky?

"Hey, if you can interpret that any other way, be my damn guest. But I think that he was being pretty clear with what he said. No double meanings that I can figure out."

Nine turns away from me. His strong profile beneath the moonlight has me wondering why I'm trying to pick a fight with him. He sighs and, for a moment, when the cloud cover passes right over the moon, I think he's fading back into the shadows.

Then the clouds roll swiftly by and Nine is still there, avoiding my earnest gaze.

"Fine," he admits. "When you were very young, I struck a bargain with a human woman to repay an old debt of mine. Your mother. I gave her my word that I would watch over you if anything ever happened to her. I have only done what I promised to do."

It's a good thing I'm sitting on the ground. I feel like I've been sucker-punched. A sense of betrayal weighs my gut down like rocks. I'm suddenly aware that I never pushed for the reasons why he constantly visited me when I was little. I took it for granted that he wanted to—not that he was forced to.

Or that, all along, he only acted on orders from a mother who wanted to keep me protected.

"And you never thought that you should tell me that?"

Nine has the nerve to look surprised, like he doesn't quite understand why I'm so upset. "Why would I?"

"She was my mother!" I explode. "You let me spend my whole life thinking she didn't want me!"

"Yes," he says softly. His calm tone just makes me angrier. "But what would knowing that have done? It won't bring Callie back."

That's it. That's the last straw. You can only take too much until you crack and, deep down, I've been a fragile mess for most of my life. I've got this tough facade, hardened over the years, but it's only that—a facade. I've been splintering for a while now.

Of everything he's said, the casual way he uses her name is it. It's enough to make me shatter.

I push up off of the ground. Pure fury burns through my fatigue. My cheeks feel like they're on fire. My hands, too. I want to push him. To shove him. To hit him and hit him and hit him until Nine knows what it feels like to hurt the way that I'm hurting now.

His betrayal cuts like a knife. Tears spring to my eyes, almost like blood on the floor.

I don't want him to see. Wiping angrily at my face, the leather burning against my skin, I storm away from him.

"Riley... Riley! Stop. Where do you think you're going?"

Without turning around, I snap back. Let the caretaker hear me. I don't give a shit.

"Me? I'm going as far away from you as I can. Look." The moon's shining high over my head. It leaves a sliver on the dirt path, shadows wafting on the borders. "Shadows. Maybe I can jump in one and I'll be back at Black Pine." I leap, landing unsteadily, one of my slippers slipping out from under me. I angrily jam my foot back inside. "Oh, well. Guess not."

Nine takes two purposeful steps closer. His entire form is tensed. He's ready to come after me if I don't listen to him.

Yeah. Let him try.

I stomp off again.

His voice follows me. "Riley. You must stay with me. Rys has his own motives, but the queen could send any of my kind after you while it's still dark."

Wow, Nine. That was absolutely the worst thing to say to me right now.

I whirl on him, shoving my hair over my shoulder so that I can focus all of my unadulterated rage on him. "And?" I shoot back. "Maybe I should stick it out and wait for him. The Light Fae told me more about what's going on in my life tonight than you did in *fifteen years*."

"Don't say that. You don't know what he's capable of. He killed your friend just to get to you."

That's a slap in the face. I recoil from his harsh words.

As if I had forgotten *that*.

It takes a second for me to recover enough to retort. "Oh, yeah. Thanks for that, by the way. I know you left me behind, but at least you could've warned me about him before he snapped my sister's neck."

"I was trying to protect you."

I clap. The leather muffles the sound. "You did an amazing job. Six years in the asylum, haphephobia, and the ugliest hands you'll ever see. Plus, Madelaine's dead. She was my sister. Why couldn't someone protect *her*?"

"There's more to it than that." Nine gentles his voice. He's trying to placate me, to keep me from flipping out entirely, saying or doing something I'll regret. It's like pouring gasoline on the raging fire of my emotions. "If you would just calm down and let me explain—"

I shake my head. No. *No*. It's too little, too late. I don't want to hear anything else he has to say. No more worthless 'explanations'. Humming out loud, I cover my ears in a bid to drown his sensible voice out. I don't care if I look crazy. After all this time, I've gotten used to it.

And then Nine does something that I'm not expecting. Moving so fast, as if he teleported from his spot to right in front of mine, he lashes his hand out, wrapping his deceptively strong fingers around my wrist.

My sleeve rides up enough for his fingertips to find a patch of my skin. It sends a shock through my entire system, making me let out one hell of a primal scream. Nine tears one hand from my ear before he yanks his arm back.

As soon as he lets go of me, I clamp my mouth shut. I throw myself backward, ducking to the grass when I see the lights in the caretaker office come blazing to life.

The door creaks open, followed by a shout.

"Who's out there? The cemetery's closed. Don't make me call the cops!"

My pulse thuds. Huddled in the grass, I shove my sleeve up, rubbing his aggressive touch from my skin. I can still feel it lingering there. I wipe at the patch, trying to erase it. Not because it's Nine or because he's a fae, but because that wasn't my choice.

The caretaker stands on the porch for a few seconds that seem like a lifetime. I can't tell if Nine slipped into the shadows and disappeared or not. I don't see him, but I'm also super focused on the open door. I shouldn't have screamed. I didn't want to involve the old man. And, sure, the cops might be able to help me —but not if I get busted for trespassing.

As soon as the caretaker decides he scared some no-good screamer off his property and heads back inside, Nine is suddenly there again.

He's cradling his right hand. Unless I'm seeing things—and my night vision is actually kinda amazing —there are these faint wisps of pale grey smoke coming from his palm. He flexes his fingers, careful to keep his hand turned toward his chest.

I'm immediately distracted from my anger. What's up with that?

I jerk my chin at him. "Aren't you going to give me a hand up?"

Nine holds out his left hand to me.

Yeah, that didn't work the way I wanted it to.

I shake my head. I definitely don't take his hand.

"Forget it. What's up with the other hand, Nine?" An eerily familiar scent drifts on the breeze. My stomach turns. I know it too well—it took months before I got it out of my nose after the fire. "Why does it smell like burning flesh?"

He doesn't say anything. Instead, his lips pulled into a thin line, Nine shows me his hand. Each finger is burned raw, red blisters on every inch of his palm.

I stare in horror.

His pale skin is utterly destroyed.

CHAPTER 14

"**W**hat the *hell*—"

Nine blinks, stretching his fingers as if he's trying to slough off the ruined skin. I want to tell him to stop. His face is completely stoic. Except for the constant stretch, he doesn't give any indication that his hand's gotta be killing him.

"And now you see why I must have your permission."

Because he touched me. Without my permission, he can't leech any power from a touch. I didn't know that it burned the shit out of *him*, though.

I think back to the recently healed skin I saw on his hand earlier. It was when we landed in Faerie, right after he grabbed me without permission in my room. I know fae have crazy fast healing abilities—it's part of their magic—but I never put two and two together before. He must've been burned then, too.

So why did he do it? Why was it so important to him that I leave the asylum? Or listen to him try to explain? He had to have known what would happen if he grabbed me when I wouldn't let him.

I'm grateful when he tucks his burnt palm back into his chest. It reminds me too much of what my hands looked like after I reached through the enchanted flames to get to Madelaine. I didn't know she was dead. I had hope, and I would've walked through fire to save my sister. She was my best friend—except for Nine— and she was normal. Even better, she treated me like *I* was normal. She didn't deserve to die.

Rys dared me to save her. I tried. I really did. I managed to push my hands through the fire that circled Madelaine's body. It was so hot. So fucking hot. It burned the skin right off my hands, the white-hot agony making it impossible for me to go any further.

I blocked out a lot of what happened next. Dealing with my grief following Madelaine's death was almost as difficult as what I went through to save my hands. The burns were so bad that I needed multiple surgeries just to get to the point where I could finally have an autograft done. Seeing Nine's injury now, my fingers start to throb in sympathy pain.

I drop my face into my hands. The leather against my skin is familiar and reassuring. I breathe in deep. It helps.

Until Nine starts to speak again.

"Listen to me." I peek at him through the slivers of space between my fingers. "You must—"

Okay. That's it.

I drop my hands.

"I'm done."

"Shadow—"

Gritting my teeth, I tell him, "Don't call me that."

"We have to get you somewhere else. A building with iron in it would work. Either up high or down below. It'll throw the soldiers off your scent and then we—"

I cut him off right there. "There is no we. I told you, Nine. I'm done. Go. Leave me the hell alone. You don't have to keep on pretending that you care what happens to me."

Nine blinks. "I'm not pretending."

He only cares because he feels like he's repaying the woman I never got the chance to meet.

"My mom told you to protect me, right?" That's what Rys said. "You said the Light Fae didn't have the power to wipe the debt clear. Do I?"

"You don't know what you're saying."

Maybe I don't. "Yes or no?"

"I'm supposed to help you. I've accepted my duty. It took me years to understand, but this is what I'm supposed to be doing. Don't do this. Not now, Shadow. Not when I know the soldiers are after you."

So that's a yes, then. Okay. "Nine, consider your debt paid in full."

His silver eyes flash. I can't tell if it's in annoyance, anger, or relief, but a dark shadow passes across his face as his glowing eyes light up his beautiful features.

He dips his right hand into the pocket of his jacket, pulling out the same rock he showed Rys. When he opens his hand, I see the rock—and I notice that his hand is almost completely healed.

"I'll go because you've asked me to, not because I consider the debt closed. I'm still clinging to the bargain, Shadow. I won't return this yet."

His rock? What the hell do I want with his rock?

"Whatever. Just go."

He nods. "If you need me, call me. I'll return to you as soon as I can."

I turn my back on him. It's tough, seeing Nine so defeated. My whole life, he was my knight in the shadows. My guardian. My protector. If this is the last time I see him, it's a shitty way to go out.

But I can't do this. I wasn't kidding when I said I'm done.

"Yeah, well, don't hold your breath."

There's no answer from behind me.

I glance over my shoulder.

Nine's already gone.

I SPEND MY FIRST NIGHT ON THE OUTSIDE *INSIDE* of a mausoleum.

I've got nowhere else to go. My first instinct was to find a way back to Black Pine and I figure out way too late that I let my trip home slip through my fingers when I forced Nine to leave.

And, sure, he might think I have this skill to shade-walk, but I'm just starting to fully accept the powers of the fae after six years of pretending they don't exist. Even though I obviously moved out of my room at the asylum, it's going to take me a minute to figure out how *that* happened.

Madelaine is buried here in Acorn Falls, a well-to-do little nook of a town about a city or two over from Black Pine. This is where the Everetts used to live before they moved more than six hours away. I lived here with them for close to two years, before the accident and the hearings and the decision that I should be kept inside of the residential ward at Black Pine until I was twenty-one.

I should know where I am and how to get back. I don't. Besides, it's the middle of the night. What can I do? I'm not gonna be able to stay here long-term, but there's no harm in staying over until morning. If I start wandering in the dark, I'll end up even more lost.

At least, that's what I convince myself as I start looking for a place to hide.

My instincts lead me to the old mausoleum that shielded me from the rain the last time I was here. The Richardsons' mausoleum is big and wide. Not too long after I sent Nine away, the caretaker left. It's just me here now. Maybe I can hide on the backside of the big mausoleum and get some sleep. I'm already exhausted. I'll never make it 'til tomorrow if I don't get some real shut-eye now.

For once, luck's on my side. After I stumble over

mounds of earth and silent graves, I see that the door is cracked open, almost as if someone has been expecting me. A thick piece of wood is wedged between the stone wall and the door, leaving just enough space for a slim person to slip inside.

I'm no Carolina, but I make it inside by holding my breathing and squeezing my way in.

The mausoleum has a strange smell, musty and chemical; considering what else is in this crypt, it could be worse. There is one questionable puddle along the far wall. I just make sure to stay on the other side, about three feet away from the wall full of caskets.

I keep my head down, figuring that, so long as I stare at the concrete floor instead of the ornate shelves, I can forget that there are dead bodies in here with me.

It's fine. I'm not afraid of the dead. The dead can't touch me.

They can't do anything to hurt me at all.

I sit cross-legged on the stone floor, running the edge of my gloves along the side of my slipper. I'm tired, sure, but I think I've gotten to the point that I'm *over*-tired. I feel like I drank two espressos, then chased it with an energy booster or something. I'm buzzing, super focused. I use the sense of touch to ground myself. Without being able to touch another person, I've gotten used to touching *me*. I run my fingers along my slipper, my calf, my knee, my arm. I'm here. I'm in one piece.

For now.

I peer at my slippers. They're damp, but still clean for the most part; flecks of dried mud cover the side and are stuck in the treads. Because I had planned on visiting Carolina, I'm not in my robe or my pajamas. I've got on my hoodie, but at least I'm also wearing an old pair of faded jeans. That'll help me out tomorrow.

For now, I'm grateful for the freezing air conditioning the Black Pine staff keeps running all year long. Even though the summer days are warm, the summer nights are chilly, so I'm kind of used to this weather. It's really cold inside of the mausoleum, though. Without my hoodie, I don't think I could have made it through the night.

Eventually, I crash. It had to happen. Even though I keep thinking I hear someone coming—Nine, Rys, the caretaker, I don't even know anymore—I drift off to sleep, curled up on the stone floor of the mausoleum.

I don't know how long I'm sleeping. It feels like it's only been a few minutes when I'm blinking myself awake again, but the air is different than it was. Thicker. Heavier.

The inside of the mausoleum isn't as gloomy, either. Light filters in through the crack in the door. I'm so happy to see it. One, because the light tells me that it's daytime. I made it through the night. And two, no one closed the mausoleum behind me. I'm not trapped in here with the dead.

No, I'm just an escapee from a glorified psych hospital. 'Cause that's so much better.

Slowly, I pull myself up into a sitting position, stretching my stiff arms and my achy legs. Apart from that, I don't really move. Moving means accepting that I have to come up with a plan to get back to Black Pine.

I never thought I'd feel homesick for the asylum. I totally do. I'd do anything to be back there right now. I'm too worried, too scared, too apprehensive to feel hungry, but that's not gonna last. I'm gonna need to eat soon.

And what about my pills? My morning meds? I can't say for sure if they actually did anything. Still, I know withdrawals are no joke. I can't just stop taking my medication and assume that everything's gonna be okay.

How long will it take before my body realizes it's missing them? I've heard horror stories about withdrawals. I'm not looking forward to it.

My head is heavy on my shoulders and I give it a few experimental rolls on my neck. My hair feels knotted and tangled as it hangs down my back. I wish I had a hair-tie or a rubber band or something to get it out of my face. I twist it and tuck it beneath my hoodie for now. Wiping my dirty gloves on my even dirtier jeans, I start to stand. I was thinking I should wait to break out again until it's a little later, maybe while the caretaker is at lunch. I don't want to risk getting caught leaving the mausoleum, but I can't sit here any longer.

I stay on the dark side of the crypt, pacing back and forth, anything to get rid of this nervous energy. My slippers pad almost noiselessly against the stone floor.

When I turn, they shuffle; apart from that, there's no sound. At least I'm used to the quiet. It's one thing that has never bothered me. I enjoy it. It's helpful, too, because when I hear the rustle coming from nearby outside, I'm not caught entirely unaware.

Not that I can do anything about it. By the time they get close enough that I realize they're heading for the open mausoleum, there's no way for me to get out first.

I freeze. Is it the caretaker? Did he finally pick up on the fact that the mausoleum is partially unsealed and he's coming to check it out? Or, worse, was the door propped open because they're getting ready to put another casket inside?

Oh, no, no, no...

A ray of golden light falls at my feet as a very tall, very beautiful fae slips gracefully inside of the crypt. Even in the dark, dank gloom, Rys seems to shine.

So, uh, not the caretaker then.

At that moment, I don't think I've ever wished to have a weapon on me more than I do now. A baseball bat, a lead pipe, anything. He's paused in the entryway, but I know that's his way of making a grand entrance.

I don't want to let him get any closer and I resort to holding up my hands to ward him off.

"Stay back," I tell him. "Don't come any closer."

Rys's gleeful laughter sends chills up and down my spine. He places one hand to his chest. "Is that how you greet your mate?"

Not this garbage again. Seriously, I think this guy

belongs in the asylum. It's as clear a case of obsessive delusions as I've ever seen. Then there's the fact that I know he can go into violent, murderous rages in one second, before laughing and smiling charmingly in the next.

I back away. One of the casket handles on this side of the crypt jams into my back, the one above it barely missing the bottom of my head. I let out a grunt of pain, though I don't take my eyes off of Rys.

"What are you doing here? How did you find me?"

"Now that you're finally coming into your power, your soul is reaching out for its mate." Rys advances on me. My breath catches in my throat. "I have the power to follow you wherever you go. You gave me that, Riley."

"I didn't give you shit!"

"Oh? Is that so?"

"Yes! You're not supposed to be here. I don't want you anywhere near me, you freak."

Rys stops on the edge of the light. The corners of his mouth turn up slightly, revealing gleaming white teeth. I can't help but notice that his canines are longer than the rest. They look like fangs.

"Unlike my kind, humans can tell an untruth. I suggest you get better at it if you want me to give up on our mating, my *ffrindau.*"

"Wait— you think I *want* you chasing after me?"

He does. I don't need to use my talent as a gauge to know that he does. This fae actually thinks that I like his attention.

What the hell?

It's like the day with Diana and her gold-colored eyes all over again. My breathing starts to quicken now, shallow breaths as I struggle to take in more and more oxygen. If I'm not careful, this could turn into one of those debilitating attacks that leaves me on the floor, sitting on my hands. I can't have that. I've gotta keep calm.

I've gotta get out of here.

Though I told myself—and him—that I didn't want his help, I find myself blurting out: "Nine!"

Rys shakes his head, long, fair hair swaying hypnotically as he paces along the line that separates the light from my dark side. He purses his lips, visibly annoyed that I've said Nine's name.

"Don't waste your breath," he says, pouting. "Nine won't come."

I hope he's wrong. I need Nine. He's the only one I can get to help me keep Rys away from me.

I try again, "Nine, I'm sorry. Please come back!"

"He can't. There are rules, Riley."

My body shivers whenever he says my name. I thought it was fear the first time I shook. Now I'm not so sure. He makes *Riley* sound so beautiful. I should hate it—and I don't.

This can't be happening.

I focus on what he just said. Because, despite Nine telling me that he would come if I call for him, he isn't here.

I glare over at the Light Fae. I'm sure that he won't

hurt me—other humans are fair game but, for the moment, as long as he wants me to, like, marry him, he's not gonna kill me or anything. I push past my terror and my conflicting emotions when it comes to Madelaine's murderer. He's the only one who seems to want me to know what's going on.

Let's go.

"What do you mean, rules?" I demand.

Rys laughs lightly. It's such a sweet, gentle laugh, and I think that's what scares me most. He's dangerous, a menace, and yet I feel myself being drawn to him. I don't understand it and I have to stop myself from leaning in toward him.

He knows what he's doing. It's why I'm pressed up against the wall of caskets. I'm stuck among the dead people in this mausoleum all because part of me kinda likes the idea of walking up to the Light Fae.

"First of all, it's daylight. The Dark Fae are crippled during the time of the sun. He can't whip up a portal and come running without his precious shadows. And even if you're lucky enough to find one, calling him Nine isn't enough. He doesn't have to respond to it—it's not his true name. It doesn't have the power."

"True name? What's that mean? Nine's not his name?"

"Not his true name. It's like how you want to be called Riley and I'm Rys. Nine chooses to be called Nine, but it's not the name that you can use to command him." He pauses. "I don't know his, but I can give you mine. I wouldn't mind being under your command."

"That's okay. I'm gonna pass."

His grin widens. "Would you like me to tell you yours?"

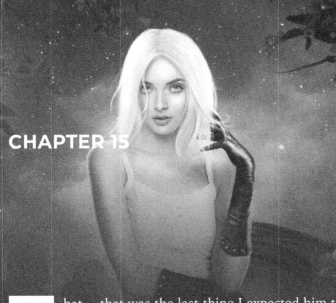

CHAPTER 15

That… that was the last thing I expected him to say. In my experience, Rys doesn't take rejection too well. The creepy grin is bad enough. But to offer to tell me *my* true name?

"What? No. I don't have a true name. I'm not… I'm not like you. I'm human."

"Mm." Rys makes a non-committal noise in the back of his throat. His golden eyes shine. "Are you so sure about that, my mate—"

"Not your mate."

He ignores me. "—that you don't have a true name? Think it over. There isn't a single name I can use that will have you doing my bidding?"

Come, Zella.

My whole body goes icy cold. That word. How many times did he use it and, suddenly, I was doing something I never would have in a million years?

213

"Come to me. Stay with me," purrs Rys. I notice he doesn't say *Zella* now. Why not? He holds out his hand. "Take my hand. Just one touch. One dance. I swear, you'll be glad you chose me. The Shadow Prophecy will ruin you, Riley. Come with me. I'll save you from the Fae Queen. If you're with me, she'll forget all about you. If you choose Nine... well, he's a Dark Fae. She'll never believe you're not the Shadow."

Choose Nine? That's the part that sticks out at me the most. Who said it was a contest between the two fae? One's a monster, the other my former protector.

"Why does that matter? That Nine's a Dark Fae and you're not?"

He beckons me toward him.

I stay where I am.

"Just one more dance," wheedles Rys. "I need the touch, and then I'll tell you everything you've ever wanted to know about Nine."

That's very tempting. For years, Nine told me everything about Faerie and the fae—but he didn't tell me a damn thing about himself. Not even his name apparently. Rys obviously has more answers that he can provide... but I can't touch him.

I can't.

It's about possession. He's making it clear that, for some reason, he wants me. That's how the fae live. They want what they want when they want it. Nine warned me of that a long time ago. When it comes to humans especially, the fae love to possess them. To take them, to charm them, to turn them into mindless slaves, to leave them, to destroy them, to forget all about them.

And it all begins with the touch.

"Dance with me. One dance," he whispers, "and we'll both have everything we've ever wanted."

I know what he's doing. He's done it before, when I was sedated and I allowed myself to believe that it was a dream. Just one dance—it's nothing but an excuse to steal another touch, to take another part of my soul.

"You killed Madelaine," I accuse him. I have to remember that. No matter what, he can't take that back. But, and I'm ashamed to admit this, my protest is half-hearted.

"I did," he agrees. "She was a means to an end. If I knew then that she actually meant something to you, I might've done things differently. You must remember, though, she was just a human."

"*I'm* a human."

"Mm. So you keep saying."

There's that noise again. He doesn't agree with me.

Okay. That's it. I'm done talking to him. If I keep on listening to what the Light Fae has to say, it won't be long before he talks me into doing whatever he wants me to. His glamour is way too strong, my defenses are weak, and I need to get my head on straight.

Something's wrong. I should be way more frightened than I am. I *should* be afraid. I'm stuck in a mausoleum with a mythical creature who murdered my sister—and now he wants me to willingly give him everything I have. Only a few days ago, seeing his eyes shining out of Diana's face put me into hysterics. I should be losing it right now.

He didn't use that *Zella* word. I don't think he needs to. I mean, he drew Madelaine to him with his beautiful smile and his lilting voice. Maybe that's exactly what he's doing to me now. He's charming me, using his glamour and his fae magic to compel me to go to him.

Once again, Rys holds out his hand expectantly. From the look on his face, I can tell that he thinks he's got me.

If that's all he wants, then that's the one thing I'm gonna make sure he doesn't get.

All I have on my side is the element of surprise. Now that I'm paying attention to it, I can almost feel his charm pulling me further toward him as another second passes. I already stepped away from the wall of caskets behind me, my slippers shuffling as I edge toward him. If I don't fight back now, I'm screwed.

I'll only have one chance. It'll be risky, but it's the only choice I have.

He waits for me in the weak stream of light. I keep thinking about how the Light Fae are powerful during the day, with the Dark Fae coming out at night. Unless I'm imagining it, Rys is purposely avoiding the shadows on this side of the mausoleum.

Guess we're gonna find out.

I move closer to him. When I'm standing on my

side of the invisible line that's separating us, Rys reaches one long finger out toward my cheek. He stops when he's a few inches away. It's like there's a barrier that he can't break through.

Know what? There probably is.

It has everything to do with these rules the fae live by. I know all about this one. I haven't given him permission to touch me, and he's not willing to get burned when he's so confident that I'll give in to him.

Giving him a meaningless smile, I sidle around him, draping my arm around his slender waist as if I'm getting in position to give him the dance he's been hoping for. Rys shivers at my purposeful touch. My stomach revolts, my skin crawling as I make contact, but I don't pull away from him until I've moved behind him.

Then, with all of the strength I have in me, I place my gloved hands on the small of his back and shove.

He wasn't expecting me to attack him. I know that. If I didn't let him think he won, didn't give him a little taste of me with the seductive stroke across his side, Rys never would've been caught off-guard like that.

I hated every second of it, but it was worth it. He never expected it and I manage to push him into the dark depths of the shadows before he even has the chance to retaliate.

I wasn't wrong when I realized he was avoiding the shadows on purpose. The second he crosses the line, Rys lets out an unholy scream of terror. The shadows streak his bronze skin, turning the deep, rich color an inky black. His eyes light up like they're on fire.

The last time I saw him do that, he let loose a stream of flames that surrounded Madelaine.

I've gotta get the hell out of here before he does it again. I race toward the slim opening of the mausoleum and, sucking in my frightened breath, I pop out on the other side.

The heavy stone door is held open by a block of wood that's been wedged underneath. I kick at it wildly, willing it to come loose. My slipper goes flying. I don't give a shit. I almost break the big toe on my right foot as I slam it into the wood on the second kick.

It works, though. Three good, strong kicks and the wood pops free. The slab slams shut with a bang that causes my ears to ache. It echoes, or maybe that's the dying whine of Rys's furious scream when he realizes that I truly have refused him.

Again.

I don't wait around to see if Rys was able to escape the tomb before the door sealed him inside. I don't even stop to see if any of the visitors to the cemetery witnessed me bursting out of the mausoleum and closing the door behind me.

With one slipper and half a prayer, I book it the hell out of there.

DON'T STOP RUNNING.

Don't look back.

Rys could be behind me. I'm not about to look. I don't want to be some horror movie cliché, getting caught by the bad guy because I was too stupid to take off when I had the chance.

The fae are a magical race. The Dark Fae can shade-walk. I saw that firsthand when Nine broke me out of the asylum. The Light Fae? If Rys's abilities are any clue, I know they can control fire. Good chance he can find a way to escape the Richardsons' mausoleum.

I'll take any lead I can get.

I haven't sprinted like this since my middle school days, and even then I half-assed running the mile. A cocktail of fear and adrenaline erases the last of his commands. I shake it off and keep running, tearing a path through the neatly tended graves. I know this cemetery. I know exactly where I am—where I have to go.

The gate isn't too far from the Richardsons' mausoleum. I'm so focused on heading right toward it, I don't even notice that I'm running right by the care-taker's office until I hear his grizzled shout behind me.

"Hey, you! Watchu doin'? You can't run in the cemetery!"

Like hell I can't.

He chases after me, but I'm already too far ahead. Still, I hear him shout, "Get back here!"

Yeah. That's gonna be a nope. I'm still kinda disori-ented. I shook off the cobwebs of Rys's compulsion magic, but the lost feeling I woke up with earlier hasn't faded yet. I'm in Acorn Falls—the cemetery proves that —but that doesn't do a thing to help me figure out how I'm going to get back to Black Pine. It's only about half an hour away by car. On foot? I don't know. Definitely a lot longer than that.

I'll figure that out later. Right now? I dash right through the open gate, heading straight because it's in front of me and that means I'm widening the gap between me and the mausoleum where I trapped Rys.

The gravel road that leads to the cemetery is uneven and rough. The sharp edges of the rocks and pebbles bite into my poor, tender bare foot. I push past the pain. Getting out of here before Rys can come after me is the only thing I'm thinking about.

I'm not a fae. I'm not like him. I don't have a true name. I *don't*. But when he says that word, when he calls me Zella, I lose my head. He's proven it enough times already. No matter the reason behind it, he can use it to command me to do whatever he wants me to. I can't let that happen.

He wants me to do the fae equivalent of 'til death do you part with him. Not gonna happen. I'd rather spend the rest of my life inside of a facility just like Black Pine than willingly tie myself to Rys.

That's the thing, though. He has the power to compel me to be his... his *ffrindau* thing. I have to get away from him until I can come up with a plan B. Sticking around, hoping Nine will take pity on me after my temper tantrum isn't gonna work, either.

Keeping pushing forward.

Don't look back.

I can't run anymore. It's pure luck I managed to hang on to this slipper. It protects my left foot as I half-hop, half-jog over the gravel path. I curl my toes against the matted fluff to keep from losing this one, too. Once I make it to the main road, I take it off and tuck it inside of my hoodie pocket. I figure, better to have no shoes on than have people wonder why I'm wearing only one slipper.

Not like I'm not gonna get a couple of odd looks already. It's the end of June, the sun shining down on me. Definitely not hoodie weather. My jeans should be fine, though they're rumpled and stained. I probably look like I just rolled out of bed or something.

Great. There goes any hope of staying under the radar.

What if someone's out searching for me? I mean, they have to be, right? Technically, I'm an escaped mental patient. They won't know how I got out—and I know they won't believe me when I try to tell them—but as soon as Penelope came to wake me up this morning, the whole asylum must've gone on high alert when they realized I was missing.

I'd like to think that the Black Pine staff would keep my disappearance in-house to save face. Too bad I know better. During my first year at the facility, one of the patients managed to slip out during visiting hour. It was madness. Absolute chaos. The staff locked down the rest of the asylum until they found her, hours later, munching on a donut at a nearby coffee shop.

She walked out because she had a craving for a jelly donut and the whole place went nuts. I've been gone for almost a whole day by now. They must be losing their minds.

I only hope that, when I make it back there, they don't hold my escape against me. It wasn't my fault—and who am I kidding? Nine's stunt has just caused me to kiss any chance of a timely release from the asylum goodbye.

Whatever. Right now? I don't care. Black Pine's kept me safe from the fae for six years. For my sanity's sake, I have to believe that Nine is being too careful. That it's still my only hope. I've gotta go back. Then they can lock me up. Throw away the key.

I don't care.

Anything to get away from Rys.

Acorn Falls is just as I remember it.

It's a small, close-knit town full of rich people. The Everetts were comfortable enough to make their home here for a while; if Madelaine had survived, I'm sure they never would've left. It's... I guess *quaint* is the best word for it. It has an honest-to-god main street called Oak Tree Road that cuts through the town, lined with a variety of shops. Most of them are local businesses: antique shops, bakeries, delis, pet stores, collectibles, and memorabilia. Stuff like that. You won't catch a McDonald's anywhere near here, though I lose count of the Starbucks after I pass my third one.

Considering it's Saturday, the streets are nowhere near as crowded as I thought they'd be. After I've been walking for almost an hour, I run into a group of rich, teenage white boys. They're loitering on a corner, sharing a single cigarette while they glower in their starched polo shirts and hundred dollar haircuts.

Typical Acorn Falls boys. When I first came to the Everetts, I had my fun with a couple of them before they began to bore the crap out of me. I was a good time to them, and they were nothing to brag about it.

I don't recognize any of the group. Doesn't matter. They're all the same. Today, when they think they're big enough to catcall at me, I stare at each of them as I stroll by, my bare feet slapping against the hot, summer sidewalk.

When I can feel the weight of their leers, I smile. Lifting my hand, I wave at them, making sure they all get a good, long glimpse at my leather glove.

I'm tired. I'm scared. My feet are killing me. I've got no shoes, a stained hoodie, ratty hair, and mud splattered all over my legs. I'm still a chick with a pretty face out on her own. There are four of them and one of me. The streets are empty. I must look like easy pickings.

My smile widens.

I've got nothing to lose.

Not one of those boys holds my gaze for more than a split second. When I've made it past them, the tallest of them stamps out the cigarette and gestures for his friends to follow after him as he leads them back the way I came.

I keep going forward.

I still haven't figured out where I'm going. I'll have to do that soon. Without any money or a phone, though, it's not gonna be easy. I tilt my head back, looking over the rooftops of the buildings that surround me on both sides. The sun's starting to set. I let out a huge sigh of relief. Once the sun's gone, that's a good ten hours or so before I'll have to worry about Rys again.

He can't come out at night.

Nine can.

He didn't answer me before, but that was because it was during the day. Right?

I'm hanging all of my hopes on it. Nine owes me. He pulled me through the shadows and left me all alone. And, sure, I did send him away. But you know what? He should've known better than to go.

Ugh.

Stupid Dark Fae.

Stupid prophecy.

Stupid queen.

Why the hell did they have to decide that I was the stupid Shadow?

I don't want any part of it. They can't make me be what they want. Besides, it's a fae thing and, whoops, I'm not a fae. Sorry.

Pick someone else. Anyone else.

Just... not me.

It's bad enough that there's no going back from this. They can start tossing blue pills down my throat and that would never be enough for me to go back to pretending that the mythical race doesn't exist. Too much has happened. For the first time in years, my eyes are fully open to the magic around me.

Even though there's been no sign of Rys since I booked it from the cemetery, I'm on high alert. I try not to make it too obvious, though. Every couple of steps, I turn my head one way, then the next, constantly aware of my surroundings. I use the shiny, reflective glass of the storefront windows to look all around me—

—and that's exactly how I find out I'm the lead story on the five o'clock news.

I was daring a quick peek inside the window of tiny, no-name, indie electronics store when I glance at the televisions propped up on display and nearly have a heart attack.

My face is staring back at me from like five different high def screens. It's an old picture, taken straight from the papers. A shot of me leaving my juvenile court hearing weeks after Madelaine's death—right before they shipped me off to Black Pine.

Six years have passed. I haven't changed that much; on the outside, at least. I gape at the image filling the screens. I remember when I was that fifteen-year-old girl. I wore my hair shorter in those days. I was tanner, too—my skin was always sun-kissed back then—and a couple of pounds heavier.

I look resigned in that picture.

I recognize the expression intimately. It's the same one I've seen in the mirror every morning since then.

I'm so consumed by the image from a lifetime ago, it takes me a second before I realize there are words plastered on the screen directly beneath the picture.

My jaws drops when I read them.

Black Pine Patient: Missing One Week

CHAPTER 16

In the glass, I see my open mouth reflected back at me. I gulp. Stare. Then, a heartbeat later, my lips move.

"A *week?*"

It comes out like a squeal. I gasp, then cover my mouth with my gloved fingers.

A perky brunette appears on the screen as my picture is minimized to a square in the upper right corner. No sound—or maybe I can't hear it through the glass, I don't know—but there are no captions, either, so I can't figure out what she's saying about me.

I only know it can't be anything good.

One week missing?

Are you kidding me?

How?

No. Seriously.

How?

I only left *yesterday*.

I don't get it. It's not... it's not possible. And I know that this is only one more impossible thing to lump in with the rest, but time is time. Seconds. Minutes. Hours. I was at Black Pine only last night and, while I slept for a little while, it wasn't like I fainted and stayed knocked out for *six whole days*.

According to the news, though, I did just that.

I don't get it. However, before I can even attempt to wrap my head around it, my senses start to ping. I catch a flash of black and white cruising toward me out of the corner of my eye. The ping turns into clamoring warning bells.

Ah, crap.

Black and white cars mean only one thing.

Ten minutes ago, I would've been relieved to see a cop car pulling up along the curb behind me. Flag it down, explain who I am, see if the cop would be willing to give me a lift back to the asylum.

I can't. Not now. If I go back, they'll want to know where I've spent the last week and I won't be able to answer them. Not can't—*won't*. And what will happen to me then?

Well, my worst suspicions were confirmed with the news report. Whether it's been one day or one week, the Black Pine staff has told everyone that I'm out here.

And, not only is Acorn Falls close enough to the asylum, but it's where I lived last. How much do I want to bet that this is one of the first places they looked?

I have to find Nine. He got me into this mess. He can get me out of it.

He *has* to.

The cop idles at the curb. I shift so that I can get a better look at him in the reflection of the glass. He's a big guy, thinning hair on top, a travel mug in his hand as he watches me through the passenger side window.

Uh-oh. Even without the shopfront acting like a mirror, I know what I look like: matted hair from the stone floor; rumpled clothes that are more suited to the cranked-up air conditioning of the facility than a summer afternoon; bare feet. And, I think with a sinking stomach, my gloves.

I shake the sleeves of my hoodie so that they cover most of my hands.

Did he see?

Tucking a strand of hair behind my ear, I move so that I'm facing away from the window. I glimpse over at the car. Not good. He traded his mug for some walkie-talkie-looking radio thing. His lips are moving while his beady eyes stay locked on me.

Shit.

Time to go.

I'm no actress, but I try. With a shocked expression and a little jerk as I shake the sleeves of my hoodie down to cover even more of my gloves, I pretend like I just remembered something super important. Then I frown, like I'm annoyed at myself. Shoving my renewed fear aside, resisting the urge to run again, I slowly walk away.

Staying calm is hard. With every casual step, my

knees shake with the need to just take off. Sure, I might get away from this cop, but what if there are more?

Don't make it suspicious, Riley. You can do this.

After I put a block between us, I give in a little. My walk turns into a speedwalk. Then, as my momentum carries me, it becomes more of a jog.

When I've made it another full block, I chance a peek over my shoulder. That's a mistake. He's still watching me and, in those few seconds, I give him a full look right at my face.

The lights flash, the air torn apart by the keening sounds of the siren as he flips it on.

I take off like a shot.

If it were any other street in Acorn Falls, he'd have had me. We're still on the main street, Oak Tree Road, so the advantage is mine. It's how it's set up. This part of the town is like a little village inside of a bigger city. Shops are built on top of shops, the wide glass windows open and inviting. Very few side streets veer off of Oak Tree, just little breaks in the road to allow people to access the back.

People, not cars.

What are my odds? I didn't get that great of a peek at the cop, but he seemed like a big guy. His hair was thinning and I'm pretty sure I saw some grey; he's older.

Come on, Riley. Think!

Would he be willing to get out of his car and chase me on foot?

I'm gonna find out.

I dart down the first opening I find, letting out a frustrated grunt when I come face to face with a five-foot-high, chainlink fence complete with a thick, metal padlock. I know why it's here. It's supposed to keep cars from trying to squeeze in between the shops to get to the alleyway behind it.

I can't let it stop *me*.

Jeez. I haven't done anything like this since I was fifteen. Sticking my battered, bruised, and bleeding bare foot into one of the holes in the fence, I grimace as the twisted iron bites into my instep before doing the same thing with the other one. I grit my teeth and climb.

Once I get to the top, I toss my body over the side. In my panic, I don't shimmy down the fence the same way I went up it. Forgetting that I'm high up in the air, I hop the fence and land *hard* on the asphalt below me.

I don't hear a snap or a crack when I hit, but my right ankles gives, then both of my knees buckle. I don't collapse in a heap or anything, but I barely stay standing. A sharp, shooting pain screams up and down my right leg before it immediately turns dull.

I hope like hell I haven't broken anything. It'll definitely make my reckless running away a bit more difficult if I have.

Shuddering out a breath, my brain whirs with a hundred different possibilities. What am I supposed to do?

I hear the sirens whine. They're getting closer. I might've been able to outrun him at first—and I was right, he didn't get out of his cop car—but this is his beat. He knows this town way better than I do. I haven't been back since I was fifteen and, even then, I only lived here for two years.

It doesn't matter if he stays on the other side of the fence. The air echoes with the sound of another siren. The alley I'm trapped in is open on this side. For all I know, he's sent out a call for help and he's got his buddy from the radio coming for me.

This alley is wider than the narrow path that led to the fence. It's designed for delivery trucks to reach the back doors of the businesses that line up along Oak Tree Road. If another cop car spots me, it'll have no problem reaching me.

But not if I'm not here for them to find.

There's a manhole a couple of feet away from the shadow of the fence. Luckily for me, the lid's not sitting where it should. Maybe the town was doing work recently on this side street and they forget to reset it. Doesn't matter. It's my only hope.

I hobble toward it, sizing up the gap. There's probably enough space for me to slip inside of it if I really try. And it's not like the cop chasing me will ever expect me to do that.

No one in their right mind would choose to go into a sewer.

Despite my stay at Black Pine, I'm not crazy. I'm not broken, either.

What I am is *desperate*.

The Fae Queen wants me dead. Rys wants me for his mate.

Nine wants to repay his stupid debt.

What do I want?

I don't know, but getting picked up by the Acorn Falls PD isn't high up there on my list. So down the manhole I go.

It's a tight fit. Tighter than when I forced my way inside of the Richardsons' mausoleum. But I want this more, and my leg hurts even worse than my tender feet. I can't run. My only choice is to hide.

I make it work.

There's a rusted ladder right inside of the entrance to the manhole. Going backward, I feel blindly with my left foot until I find it. It's slimy and cold, and I hate the idea of putting my foot on the pitted piece of metal.

I do it anyway.

Unlike the mausoleum, the sewer smells exactly the way I thought it would. Once I'm all the way inside of the dark, dank hole, I hang onto the ladder with one arm so I can pull my hoodie up and over my nose. It doesn't help. I swallow roughly, fighting back a gag. It's a good thing I haven't had a thing to eat since last night's stew. I feel like I'm about to hurl.

Or maybe that's because I'm so damn afraid that the cop is going to find me. I don't even know for sure that he recognized me as Riley Thorne, the missing girl from the news. He might've gotten a good look at me and figured rightly that I was in deep shit.

Of course, now he's got to know that I'm not innocent.

Innocent people don't run from the cops.

My queasy stomach lurches when I hear the sirens approaching. They grow louder and louder, then suddenly die. The hum of an engine not too far away replaces it. The slam of a car door. Jingling keys, and the heavy steps of an overweight police officer.

A loud huff.

I close my eyes and will my heart to slow down. It's racing so fast, beating so loud, I almost expect him to follow the thud and the thump to my hiding place. My fingers sting from clutching the ladder rung in front of me so tightly. I'm pressed up against the structure, leaning on my good leg.

This is it. Any second now he's going to realize that there's nowhere else I could go...

The crackle of his police radio cuts through the tension. I just about stop breathing. My pulse pounds. I can't understand the muttering and hiss that follows the crackle. It's too indistinct to make out from inside of the manhole.

The officer has no problem. He responds with a low growl that carries. "No. No sign of her on this side." A sound like ringing bells. I think he just kicked the fence. "She had to have run out on your end."

Some more static.

"Yeah. No shoes on, like I said. Black sweatshirt. Jeans. Leather gloves, too. Looks just like the picture they sent over last week."

The other cop says something else. I wish I could hear it.

"Look, I'll meet you over on Elm. She's fled Oak Tree on foot so that's our best chance. We can fan out, hit downtown again." Another burst of static, then, "Yeah. Copy that. I'm on my way."

His keys jingle a little faster as he moves away. The cop pounds the pavement back, his steps fading the further he gets from the fence. A minute later, the sudden roar of the engine causes the ladder to tremble. I don't pry my gloves from my tight hold until the only thing I can hear is the soft tinkling of the water trickling far beneath me.

Gritting my teeth, I start to climb down. I've got no choice. If the cops are up here looking for me, then I'm going down until I can get my head on straight and figure out just what I should do next.

The ladder goes all the way to the bottom. There's a ledge down here, overlooking a groove in the sewer. It looks like it was built to hold a small river or something but, thank God, there's nothing more than a trickle of a foul-smelling liquid.

Great. Looks like I found the source of the stink.

I don't get too close, moving as far away from it as I can until my back is against the slimy brick wall. Then, because there's nowhere else to go—and I'm beginning to ache all over—I sit on the edge of a puddle of something thick and oily. When the sliver of light from up above hits it, I see a rainbow. It's a spot of something beautiful in this terrible place.

I almost have to laugh.

At least I'm safe. For now, I might be alone, but I'm safe.

I don't plan on staying down here long. Just long enough to catch my breath, maybe, and to give my sore leg some rest. Sooner or later, I'm going to have to think about food—my anxiety makes me lose my appetite, but I'm already feeling weaker than I usually do. And I'm not about to sleep in a sewer.

I have to draw the line somewhere.

I keep my eyes squinted until I get used to the darkness surrounding me. I can't see much more than what's in front of me. The sliver of light is enough for me to be sure that I'm alone. No rats. No alligators. No—

The light sparks. It goes from a weak stream to a blinding flash. I shriek and throw my hands up as if that's going to save my poor retinas.

Out of nowhere, I hear a thunk and a slapping noise from right next to me. The splash of that dirty, oily water as it sprays up and cuts right through my jeans is chilly and uncomfortable. My eyes sting, but they fly open anyway. I blink rapidly, trying to get my sight back, then swallow my terrified squeal when I see what it was that caused the splash.

There, lying on its side in the puddle as if it's been tossed at me, is the slipper I lost in the mausoleum.

AUTHOR'S NOTE

Thank you for reading *Asylum*!

This series is one that's close to my heart. I wrote the first draft of what would eventually be one part of *Favor* (the series prequel available now) and *Asylum* back in 2013 a shortly after a close family member was inside of a facility fairly similar to Black Pine.

I came up with the idea of Riley, a poor girl who fell in with the fae, and who ended up in a facility because no one believed her. Of course, as you see in this first book, she was right—the fae are real, and they're coming for her.

Good thing she has Nine to help her navigate through this strange new world she's forced to face. Well, if she *lets* him, that is.

This is the first book in Riley's story. Now that she's out of the asylum, the adventure is only just beginning. Don't forget to turn the page and check out the next book's cover and blurb, as well as a sneak peek at *Shadow*!

xoxo,
Jessica

SHADOW

SNEAK PEEK AT THE
SECOND BOOK

He *tsks*. "Riley. Do take care of yourself."

If I didn't know better, I'd almost think he gave a shit about me.

I glare over at him. It's hard, since he's so bright and the sewer is dark, and I can barely make out the self-satisfied smile tugging on his pouty lips, but I refuse to let him think I'm happy to see him.

"How did you do that?" I demand.

"Do what, my love?"

The denial is immediate. "I'm not your love."

"Mmm. Yet, perhaps." His golden eyes glow so vividly, I have to squint to keep from being further blinded myself. "What did you mean? Do what?"

I wave my hands, gesturing at the space in front of him before shielding my gaze again. "You weren't here. You *weren't*. And then, all of a sudden, you were right next to me. How the hell did you do that?"

"I could tell you, even teach you the same skill, but…"

"Yeah?"

Rys shrugs. "It would cost you."

It would. And I can't afford his price. "No, thanks."

"A trade, then?" His voice gentles, like it's an off-handed suggestion. His expression gives him away, though. In that moment, I could ask for anything and he would give it to me. That kind of power is heady, even if I don't want anything to do with the Light Fae. "I know I'll have to earn another touch. I understand the game. But what about a barter?"

That's probably worse. A fae can't lie, I know that much, however the Faerie races are so tricky, he could be telling me the absolute truth—and still be manipulating me.

Like now. Even though I like to think I know better, I can't stop myself from saying, "I don't have anything you want. And a touch is off the table. No way am I letting you get any closer to me."

"Fair enough. As for your end, why don't you let me decide whether you have something that suits me. So, is it a deal? Do you we have an accord?"

He's gotta be kidding, right? "No."

Rys laughs.

The sound sends shivers coursing through me.

"Do you know?" he says cheerfully. "You're the first soul in more than a century who has said no to me—and now you've done it repeatedly. It's so… so *refreshing.* Ah, Riley. And you wonder why I love you so and desire you as my *ffrindau.*"

Forget shivers. My blood runs *cold*. No way I've forgotten what that fancy foreign word means. soulmate. Madelaine's killer is still insisting that I'm supposed to be his bride or something like that.

That's why he keeps running after me. Chasing behind me. Not because the Fae Queen is making him, but because he's convinced that *me*—a human orphan on the run from the asylum—and *him*—an ageless mythical creature with powers I can't understand—are somehow meant to be.

Yeah, no.

Not. Gonna. Happen.

I pull myself up off the nasty sewer floor, backing into the dark shadows so that I'm almost hidden. Rys sees me. The way his unearthly beautiful face follows my every move, it's impossible to really hide, but I feel better being cloaked in the darkness.

And, okay, maybe knowing the ladder is right by my hand makes me feel a little better. I've got no shot at beating him up the ladder. I learned long ago that the golden fae is as fast as he is vicious and cruel.

I have to remember that.

My hand closes on the rung nearest to me. "How did you know where to find me?"

"It was obvious. You're the Shadow."

I'm so sick and tired of the two fae telling me that. I don't *want* to be this Shadow person, and I'm still not too sure exactly what they expect of me except that I'm "destined" to off the Fae Queen.

Somehow, I don't think that that's what Rys is talking about right now.

"What do you mean?"

"The mausoleum. This"—he wrinkles his perfect, perfect nose—"sewer. The pockets call to you. You instinctively search them out. It was only a matter of following them to you. And here I am."

I still don't get it. "What's a pocket?"

He waves his hand toward me, toward the darker side of the sewer. I mean, the whole thing's pretty dark. It's a pit down here. But as he gestures a little further to my right, I suddenly see... something.

It's a patch that seems impossibly black, like a spot of starless night that no light can reach.

That's just at a quick glance, though. The longer I stare at the patch, the more it seems to change. It sparkles. Shimmers. Gleams.

Invites.

I edge closer to it. I don't even realize that I've moved until my glove slips off of the rung when I get too far away from the ladder.

"That's right. I'm sure you won't mind if I stay over here. The pockets belong to the Cursed Ones." Rys turns sharply, spitting behind him. "They make shadow travel between the worlds possible for the Dark Fae and only belong to the night. For one of my kind, they're almost as bad as iron."

That... actually makes sense to me.

AVAILABLE NOW

SHADOW (TOUCHED BY THE FAE #2)

The fae are after me all because I'm the Shadow. But what the hell is *that* supposed to mean?

Black Pine Facility for Wayward Juveniles. The *asylum*. I always thought it was a place for broken kids like me and it is, I guess. But that's not *all* it is.

It's also a place where the fae put troublesome humans to forget about them.

After I was blamed for my sister's death, I was trapped inside for more than six years. My doctors—my captors—told me that I'd be free on my next birthday. In a couple of weeks, I would walk out of Black Pine forever. I believed them, too.

The fae can't lie, but that doesn't mean they tell the truth. On my twenty-first birthday, I *would* be leaving the asylum... only because the Fae Queen has decided it's time I was finally brought to Faerie to face her.

Yeah. That's, uh, that's gonna be a hard pass.

You see, I spent the last six years pretending that the fae don't exist. That all changes when a Dark Fae helps me break out of the asylum. Nine. The Shadow Man who was my loyal guardian and only friend when I was a little girl. Now that he's back in my life for the first time in years, he swears he only wants to help me.

Right.

Just like the Light Fae Rys swears he only wants to love me, even after the Fae Queen sent him to hunt me down in the name of some stupid prophecy.

Now that I'm out of the asylum, my only goal is to escape the fae chasing me. Even Nine. *Especially* Nine. And that's way harder than I thought it would be. He's... he's *different* than the Shadow Man I remember from my childhood. The cold, emotionless fae is showing me a whole new side to him—and this sexy, devoted fae is helping me discover exactly who I am inside, and who I'm meant to be.

Abandonment issues, right? I have them in spades. So while I'm trying to escape the fae, I'm also trying to outrun my growing feelings for Nine.

The prophecy says that the Shadow is destined to form a bond with a Dark Fae in order to take down the Fae Queen. If I'm supposed to be the Shadow, is Nine the Dark Fae?

One thing for sure: I'm not about to stick around and find out.

**Shadow is the second book in a planned trilogy featuring a wary & independent half-fae heroine, the Dark Fae who has shadowed her her entire life, and her quest to learn about who she really is and why the powerful Fae Queen wants her dead.

Get it now!

AVAILABLE NOW

GLAMOUR EYES (WANTED BY THE FAE #1)

She doesn't want anything to do with the fae... too bad that won't stop *him*.

Callie Brooks has a gift, though that's not exactly what she calls it. She *sees* things—has been able to since she was a little girl—and it's more of a nuisance than anything else. But so long as she pretends that she can't, she's safe. The strange creatures won't bother her if she keeps herself from staring. After more than twenty years, she's gotten pretty good at it, too. Nothing surprises her any more.

Until she sees *him*.

Aislinn is a Light Fae. One of the Seelie, and a member of the Fae Queen's guard. After a foolish mistake inadvertently offends Melisandre, the queen punishes Ash by moving his guard post to the human world.

It's an insult, but he accepts the post in the Iron because it's better to be bored than to be another statue in Melisandre's garden—or worse. What's a decade or two of human watching so long as he gets to keep his head?

Cloaked in glamour, no one is supposed to know he's crossed over. Which is why he's so... so *interested* by the curious human who seems to watch him back— and whose pretty blue eyes can see right through his glamour.

The fae trick humans. They use them. They touch them, then discard them. Ash always thought he was like the rest of his kind.

Now? He's a fae who *wants* a human, and will stop at nothing to figure out what it is about Callie that makes him—and her—different than the rest... especially when he decides to seduce her and she rejects him outright.

That only makes him want him more. And hopefully he can convince Callie to agree to accept his touch before the Fae Queen realizes that his attention has wavered, otherwise it won't be Ash who gets punished this time.

It'll be *Callie*.

****Glamour Eyes** *is part one of a duet featuring the very human Callie and the Light Fae male who will give up everything to have her...*

Out now!!

STAY IN TOUCH

Interested in updates from me? I'll never spam you, and I'll only send out a newsletter in regards to upcoming releases, subscriber exclusives, promotions, and more:

Sign up for my newsletter here!

By signing up today, you'll receive two free books!

ABOUT THE AUTHOR

Jessica lives in New Jersey with her family, including enough pets to cement her status as the neighborhood's future Cat Lady. She spends her days working in retail, and her nights lost in whatever world the current novel she is working on is set in. After writing for fun for more than a decade, she has finally decided to take some of the stories out of her head and put them out there for others who might also enjoy them! She loves Broadway and the Mets, as well as reading in her free time.

JessicaLynchWrites.com
jessica@jessicalynchwrites.com

ALSO BY JESSICA LYNCH

Welcome to Hamlet

You Were Made For Me*

Don't Trust Me

Ophelia

Let Nothing You Dismay

I'll Never Stop

Wherever You Go

Here Comes the Bride

Tesoro

That Girl Will Never Be Mine

Welcome to Hamlet: I-III**

No Outsiders Allowed: IV-VI**

Holidays in Hamlet

Gloria

Holly

Mirrorside

Tame the Spark*

Stalk the Moon

Hunt the Stars

The Witch in the Woods

Hide from the Heart

Chase the Beauty

Flee the Sun

Curse the Flame

The Other Duet**

The Claws Clause

Mates*

Hungry Like a Wolf

Of Mistletoe and Mating

No Way

Season of the Witch

Rogue

Sunglasses at Night

Ghost of Jealousy

Broken Wings

Born to Run

Uptown Girl

Ordinance 7304: I-III**

Living on a Prayer**

The Curse of the Othersiders

(Part of the Claws Clause Series)

Ain't No Angel*

True Angel

Night Angel

Lost Angel

Touched by the Fae

Favor*

Asylum

Shadow

Touch

Zella

The Shadow Prophecy**

Imprisoned by the Fae

Tricked*

Trapped

Escaped

Freed

Gifted

The Shadow Realm**

Rejected by the Fae

Glamour Eyes

Glamour Lies

Forged in Twilight

House of Cards

Ace of Spades

Royal Flush

Claws and Fangs

(written under Sarah Spade)

Leave Janelle*

Never His Mate

Always Her Mate

Forever Mates

Hint of Her Blood

Taste of His Skin

Stay With Me

Never Say Never: Gem & Ryker

* prequel story

** boxed set collection

Made in the USA
Las Vegas, NV
05 April 2025

20594434R00156